# Bound By The
# Christmastide
# Moon

# Christina
# McKnight

# PRAISE FOR CHRISTINA MCKNIGHT'S NOVELS

## *THE THIEF STEALS HER EARL*

"When I started reading this book I could not put it down...it caused another book-hangover for me. I wanted to see how things would go when the truth of Judith came out and how Simon was going to handle it...loved it."-*Sissy's Book Review*

"Jude and Cart's story is such a delight! So refreshing to see the hero shy, socially awkward and not super wealthy. I love it...This was definitely one of the best books I've read this summer." -*Reviews from a Thrifty Mom*

## *FORGOTTEN NO MORE*

"This author has made me love historical romance again." -*TwinsieTalk Book Reviews*

## *HIDDEN NO MORE*

"The storyline was really good, the writing was great. So smooth and engaging, I was able to zip right through the story, it flowed so well. I love finding new to me authors and with this wonderfully written story by Ms. McKnight I've found a new historical romance author."-*Bound by Books*

## *CHRISTMAS EVER MORE*

"*Christmas Ever More* was a wonderfully written festive novella full of hope, renewal, love, and new beginnings. If you're a fan of Christina's Lady Forsaken series, this is a must. Even if you aren't caught up, this stands well enough on its own to be a lovely addition to your holiday reading list."-*Literal Addiction*

# Books By Christina McKnight

*The Undaunted Debutantes Series*
The Disappearance of Lady Edith
The Misfortune of Lady Lucianna
The Misadventures of Lady Ophelia

*Lady Archer's Creed Series*
Theodora
Georgina
Adeline
Josephine

*Craven House Series*
The Thief Steals Her Earl
The Mistress Enchants Her Marquis
The Madame Catches Her Duke
The Gambler Wagers Her Baron

*A Lady Forsaken Series*
Shunned No More
Forgotten No More
Scorned Ever More
Christmas Ever More
Hidden No More

*Standalone Titles*
The Siege of Lady Aloria, a de Wolfe Pack Novella
A Kiss at Christmastide
For the Love of a Widow
Earl of St. Seville
The Lady Loves a Scandal
Bound by the Christmastide Moon
Bedded Under the Christmastide Moon

# DEDICATION

*For Marc ~*
*Luck brought us together…but LOVE binds us.*

# ACKNOWLEDGMENTS

A huge thank you to my fellow authors; Erica Monroe, Ava Stone, Amanda Mariel, Dawn Brower, and Deb Marlowe. Together we created an amazing anthology—and I couldn't dream of a better group of women to call friends.

There are so many people who support my passion for writing. Here are a few I am blessed to call friend: Marc McGuire, Lauren Stewart, Erica Monroe, Amanda Mariel, Debbie Haston, Angie Stanton, Theresa Baer, Ava Stone, Roxanne Stellmacher, Laura Cummings, Dawn Borbon, Suzi Parker, Jennifer Vella, Brandi Johnson, and Latisha Kahn. Thank you all for accepting me for, well, me.

A very special thank you to my editor, Chelle Olson with Literally Addicted to Detail, your skill and professionalism surpass all that I expected. Chelle Olson can be contracted by email at literallyaddictedtodetail@yahoo.com.

And to my proofreader, Anja, thank you for embarking on yet another journey with me.

Cover design and wraparound cover design credit to Sweet 'N Spicy Designs.

Finally, thank you for supporting indie authors.

# PROLOGUE

*Ditchley Hall, Southampton, England*
*June 1811*

SILAS ANSON, THE eighth Earl of Lichfield, glared across the vast, disorderly expanse of what he'd recently come to view as *his* desk, not the unfamiliar, cluttered stretch of flat surface that had once belonged to his father.

A man he barely remembered and could not conjure in his mind.

On the receiving end of Silas's scowl was none other than Mr. Horace Peabody, Esquire.

The solicitor had also come with the Lichfield title and estate.

Though Silas silently debated which was of lesser value to him: his non-existent heritance or his father's trusted advisor.

"You are telling me—" Silas clamped his mouth shut, pondering and discarding his next statement as overly crass and unwarranted, no matter the validity of it. "You are telling me I was summoned back to England, ripped from my home in France, to inherit a title and estate so entrenched in debt that ruination can only be staved off for a month's time?"

Mr. Peabody, who surprisingly in no way resembled a pea of any sort, stared mutely at Silas from behind his rounded spectacles, his hands clenched on the stack of folders in his lap. Did the man realize how cliché he appeared? Glasses, ink-stained fingers, nerves so frazzled he shook, and the piles of paperwork. Lord above, the man had arrived with an entire forest's worth of the stuff. One could only imagine the mines exploited to collect the graphite needed to scribble all the nonsense that'd been presented to Silas.

And the solicitor had appeared anxious since his arrival.

"This plan you've so graciously detailed for me is the only viable option you have been able to ascertain for rescuing the Lichfield name?" Silas needed to hear Peabody verbalize his recommended course one last time; but the solicitor only nodded, his glasses slipping down the bridge of his nose. Silas wondered if he shouldn't seek other counsel in this matter—and every matter to come. "My estate is bankrupt, the title worthless, and my only recourse—if I refuse to throw myself at the mercy of my mother's family—is as outlined on this single sheet of paper?"

To further punctuate the absurdity of the situation, Silas retrieved the aforementioned document with its hastily written paragraph and held it high for Peabody to inspect.

"That is, indeed, my recommendation, my lord," Peabody croaked, bowing his head.

If his father were not solidly in his grave, Silas would do away with the previous earl himself.

Bloody damnation, but Silas—along with his mother and siblings—had been content and otherwise entertained in Paris all these years. That was before he'd been unceremoniously summoned back to his father's homeland to usurp a title he'd never thought to possess.

Silas slumped in his seat and scrubbed his face, attempting to gain some clarity on the situation—yet, it eluded him still.

His mother, Mary Louisa Anson, Lady Lichfield, had absconded from England over fifteen years prior, her three young children in tow, never to see her husband again. Edmond Anson hadn't come looking for his family, hadn't sent so much as a messenger to check on their whereabouts or safety, nor the authorities to return his offspring to their rightful place in England.

As the years passed and no one came for them, Silas and his siblings adjusted to life in France as their mother pursued her passion for art. He'd assumed his father had forged a new life and continued as if his twin sons and young daughter had never existed.

The solicitor perked up, a new spark of hope lighting his otherwise lackluster stare. "You can always reach out to Mrs. Hambly. I have heard she is a fair woman who loves her relations. Do not so readily cast her—and your other aunts—aside. Perhaps the Countess of Somerton will be willing to step in and assist—"

Silas snorted. Yes, he'd been regaled with tales of the formidable Regina, his mother's sister, for years, and none of them spoke to her fair nature or love for her family, but rather to her need to be in control. "If my aunt cared a whit for her *relations,* she would have pursued my mother and offered assistance. Yet, my siblings and I lived on little more but stale bread and broth for years, residing above a butcher's shop in an unsavory part of Paris." Silas would not go into detail about the horrid conditions of his childhood—not with this man, at least. "No, that is not an option, at least not at this juncture."

"My plan will only solve a fraction of your problems, my lord." Peabody sighed, glancing toward the closed door of the study, his wide stare begging for any interruption as a means for escape. "And the solution itself is only temporary, at best."

"How could my father allow his estate to fall into such shambles?" Silas mused, expecting no answer, for any retort would not satisfy him.

"Because he was heartbro—" The solicitor's words cut short, and he swallowed. The tall clock chimed four times, echoing through the cavernous corridors of Ditchley Hall. "If there is nothing else you require, I will see myself out and prepare to depart for London."

Peabody stood, his lean, lanky body spoke of a man trapped behind a desk in a moldy room for over half his day, his pale skin in desperate need of sunlight.

Silas wanted the man gone, out of his office and away from Ditchley altogether. Away before word traveled to his siblings about the dire state of their affairs. Yet, that would not improve his family's situation nor hold the creditors at bay for long.

"Sit." His command reverberated off the walls and shook the windowpanes, sending a shiver down his spine. That was one positive of Ditchley Hall: his voice was a fearsome sound in every room. "I wish to speak further about my course for the next several months if I entertain your plan."

Regaining his seat, the solicitor shuffled through his folders in search of something, likely the means to keep Silas's wrath at bay a bit longer.

"An arranged marriage…"

"Yes, Lord Lichfield," Peabody nodded. "My notion to rescue the estate—at least for the time being—and keep your name and that of your siblings from the gossip mills, is to secure a mutually beneficial match."

"Mutually beneficial?" Silas had never envisioned himself wedded, especially after his parents' disastrous match. The only ones to suffer were the children of Edmond and Mary Louisa Anson. "What have I to offer a woman with a healthy enough dowry to sustain Ditchley Hall and provide for my siblings' immediate futures?"

Silas was speaking in questions once again, yet, when a man had no answers of consequence, all that was left was questions.

His entire life since fleeing England had been about finding answers...solutions to the many looming problems that plagued his family. When his mother had embraced her creative ways once across the Channel and neglected her children's upbringing, it had been up to Silas to find the means to educate his siblings, Slade and Sybil. He'd spent countless hours at the *Bibliothèque nationale de France,* first teaching himself to read, and then returning to their meager flat with the tomes necessary to instruct his brother and sister.

"You have a generations-old—and might I add, respected—title with connections to far more powerful members of society." Peabody recited the line as if he'd practiced it the entire journey from London. "That being said, I do not think it wise, or advantageous in your precarious position, to speak of the strained ties between you and your most notable relations."

Silas fairly growled. "Do you think me foolish enough to begin every conversation with the scandalous details of my mother's banishment?"

The solicitor's gaze swung back to Silas, his brow furrowed. "Your mother—errr, Lady Lichfield—was not banished. Has never been spoken of in anything but the highest regard by my employer, I mean to say, the previous Lord Lichfield...your father." Peabody held up a single finger as he riffled through his papers once more. "Ah, yes, here it is. Your father commissioned this letter in the event that your mother returned to England after his death. It states that in accordance with British law, she is, always has been, and will remain, Lady Lichfield. While you are the Lichfield heir, your mother is entitled to a hefty allowance and an estate, if she so chooses to accept it."

Chooses to accept it.

Most peculiar phrasing, indeed.

"I'm assuming this has the stipulation that it is only enforceable after my father's death." The statement drew another uneasy glance from the solicitor, and bloody hell if Silas wasn't remorseful over his lack of enthusiasm to review the piles of paperwork littering his desk. "Because there is no other reason *my father* would have allowed his *family* to live in squalor in Paris if there were funds and property set aside for my mother."

The solicitor once again focused on the folder before him, flipping pages until he found what he searched for. He lowered his head further, his lips moving as he read. "There is no such clause, my lord."

"Then why—" Silas stopped himself once more, knowing his fury would find no peace by harming the messenger. There was little use demanding to understand the inner workings of his late father. "Let us return to your original plan."

"Very good, my lord." The man's head bobbed up and down, obviously aware he'd avoided Silas's displeasure for the time being. "I have it all written down before you."

"Yes, however, there seems to be one crucial flaw."

"Oh?" the solicitor asked, leaning forward over his stack of papers to see the page on Silas's desk. "What would that be?"

Silas snatched the document and held it before him. "It details my need to wed—and marry for a healthy dowry—however, it does not purport *whom*, precisely, I should espouse." When the solicitor remained silent, he continued. "Being new to society, you should be well *aware* I am blissfully *unaware* of whom, exactly, has a sizeable dowry—and who will only bring increased hardship to the Lichfield name."

"I would never seek to command you in whom to wed, my lord."

Odd, as the man had sent numerous correspondences about what was needed to keep the earldom afloat for another quarter.

Silas massaged his temples as he eyed the solicitor.

Would anyone truly miss the incompetent man if he were not to make it back to London?

Yet, he must needs remember he was in England once more, not the uncivilized country of France—as most Englishmen were fond to classify those who chose to live across the Channel.

"By chance have you any *suggestions* for proper, financially well-endowed ladies I should seek to court?"

Peabody broke into a broad smile as if Silas had finally asked the exact question he'd been waiting to hear. "I happen to have a client who—"

"How very fortunate…"

"Yes, well, he is not actively seeking a marriage for his daughter but has sought my advice on several occasions in regards to finding a match for her."

"Her worth?"

"Pardon?" Peabody said with a gulp.

"What is her worth? If I am to sell myself to the highest bidder, I would know the reward is sufficient to see me through for several years." Silas would never entertain a union unless he reaped adequate benefits: funds enough to see his siblings accepted into society, and prestige to overshadow his mother's estranged family. "Also, I suppose I should hear what you know of the girl."

"Her dowry is sufficient if you adhere to my other advice on managing your estate and investing in appropriately modest ventures. The woman in question is the only daughter of a marquess—a wealthy and connected marquess. If you have aspirations for the House of Lords, he will be an admirable advocate."

"I have never seen myself as a political man."

"Then, perhaps, you will be more in line with her brother. He is an earl and quite the man about town. A confirmed rakehell with an untouchable reputation in business, and a propensity for the gaming tables."

This earl seemed more suited as a friend for Slade, as opposed to an ally for Silas. "I would have the family name."

"The Marquess and Marchioness of Blandford." The solicitor again searched his paper, his finger running down the page until he found what he sought. "Their daughter, aged eighteen summers, is Lady Mallory Hughes."

Silas only hoped the woman did not have a third eye—or worse, the facial hair of a man. Silas supposed the son of a flighty countess could not expect much on his return to England, and the advantages of the match certainly outweighed the negatives. He needed money and means to see him and his siblings settled among the *ton*. Things that his father hadn't seen fit to provide.

"You will handle the paperwork?" Silas inquired, his brow rising in challenge.

"Without a doubt, my lord." Peabody pushed to his feet again, clutching his folders to his narrow chest as the stack threatened to escape and cascade to the floor. "I will write him at once upon my return to London. I am certain he will entertain the match."

Silas remained seated as Peabody scurried from the room. Odd a man of such height and thin frame could scurry, but that he did. With any luck, the solicitor would arrive in London and secure the proper paperwork within a fortnight.

The grandfather clock chimed once more—five loud gongs, echoing through the house, reminding Silas he was to meet his siblings in the grand hall for supper.

# CHAPTER 1

*Bocka Morrow, Coast of Cornwall, England*
*December 19, 1811*

LADY MALLORY HUGHES gazed out the carriage
window at the passing landscape—rolling seaside hills
ending in rocky cliffs that plunged into the Atlantic
Ocean—and marveled at the awe-inspiring sense of it
all. Having visited Tetbery Estate numerous times over
the years, Mallory was still awestruck by the beauty of
the region.

However, this trip to Cornwall was far different
than her previous visits. Mallory relished a few days
spent with her dear friends, Felicity, who called Tetbery
home, and Tressa, the vicar's daughter. However, the
true purpose of her visit to Cornwall was far less
enjoyable, and the main reason her Aunt Hettie had
been sent as her chaperone.

"Mallory?" Lady Hettie's gruff voice called from
across the carriage. "Child, I swear your father is right to
worry over you."

She brought her stare to Lady Henrietta Hughes—
or Hettie as the woman was called by one and all—

where she sat, her hunched shoulders appearing almost painful, and her swollen knuckles white where her hands were clasped in her lap. Any irritation Mallory might have felt—which she most certainly did not feel— would have dissipated at the sight of the older woman.

Despite her peculiar ways, Aunt Hettie loved her.

Precisely because Hettie was peculiar, as well.

"Do you worry over me?" Mallory questioned, assessing her aunt's reaction in the shifting color of her grey eyes. Irises that Mallory need remember she shared with her aunt—her emotions as vivid and stark in her gaze as Hettie's. "Do you not think I can care for myself?"

Hettie shook her head, her stringy, brown hair shot through with grey falling over her shoulder. "It has naught to do with your ability to care for yourself but your need to care for those around you."

Very accurate, Mallory mused.

"Was your father right to be worried?" Hettie prodded as their carriage shifted, turning on to the long drive that would lead to Felicity's home at Tetbery Estate.

"It is not my fault I see an obligation to speak when my gift presents itself." She would not apologize for who she was. "I do not understand how you keep such things to yourself."

Hettie smiled, revealing her slightly crooked but pearly white teeth. "Speaking of that which I see does no one any good, my child. What shall be, shall be."

It had been the debate between them since Mallory came to understand and accept her gift—or curse, as her older brother, Adam, called it. As if she and her aunt were common witches who brewed steaming concoctions in caldrons to hex those who angered them.

It did not work that way. Although, Mallory would be hard-pressed to deny she'd dreamed many times of placing a curse on her brother. Not because of his normalcy—she had never longed to be normal—but due to his views on those who did not fit into society's mold for acceptable behavior.

Thank the heavens they were arriving at Tetbery Estate, and the long journey to London was not necessary.

Tetbery was the one place Mallory could be herself without fear of judgment or admonishment. She need make no excuses for her visions, nor fear them overtaking her as was common. "As your father has commanded, you will speak of your visions to me and only me during our stay at Tetbery." Her aunt gathered her book and shawl from the bench seat as she spoke, quickly shoving them into her satchel. "That is unless it is your wish to end your betrothal."

Mallory turned back toward the window, spotting Felicity sitting upon a fallen timber, her gaze on their carriage as it drew near. "I have given my word that I will in no way jeopardize the agreement my father made with Lord Lichfield—unless I find the man unacceptable."

"Very good, my child," Hettie mumbled. "Though, if you decide that remaining unwed better suits, I will support that decision, as will my brother."

Yes, Mallory had long believed her aunt—more a mother figure to her—would back any decision she made for her future as long as it did not include joining a Gypsy tribe and using her gift to raise coin.

The life of a spinster was not for Mallory. A fact she'd known her entire life. She wanted a family, a husband and children, and did not believe her visions excluded her from that, despite the rare glimpse of her future she'd gotten, showing Mallory's fate following the path of spinsterhood. Adam would not prove as kind and accommodating to his spinster sister as Mallory's father had been to Hettie.

"We have arrived—" Hettie's words cut short as the carriage halted. "But there is a man present. He looks to be a stuffy lord, if I've ever seen one. When is

Lord Lichfield expected to call on us?"

Mallory pressed close to the glass to gain a proper look at the man. "Father said he would send word to Tetbery when he arrived. He is in Cornwall for his cousins' weddings and will take an afternoon to meet with us."

The carriage door opened to reveal Felicity below.

As was proper, Aunt Hettie was handed down first, though Mallory dearly desired a hug from her friend.

"Dear girl," Aunt Hettie greeted, placing a quick kiss to Felicity's cheek before stepping back to appraise the woman. "You become more beautiful with each passing year."

Another fact Mallory could not deny. Womanhood suited her friend well. Her untamable red hair now hung in perfect curls, and the blossom in Felicity's cheeks was something altogether new. Her friend was happy, something Mallory hadn't seen since the woman's guardian had passed away some months before.

The footman reached up to hand Mallory down, and a joyful smile broadened Felicity's already happy demeanor. Surely, Mallory mirrored the woman's delight.

Mallory pointedly kept her focus on Felicity, not risking a glance to the man who stood several paces away. If Lord Lichfield were going to disregard their agreed upon stipulations for their first meeting, she would not give him the satisfaction of her notice.

However, Mallory's intended cut did not meet its mark as the man strode forward. "I am Nicholas Harding, Duke of Wycliffe. Please allow me to welcome you to Tetbery Estate."

Her attention instantly snapped to the man. Not Silas Anson, the Earl of Lichfield, but the man who rightfully possessed Tetbery Estate. She'd often wondered after the man who took such great pleasure in gaining Felicity's wrath.

Hettie let loose an unladylike snort. "We have been

here many times before, and never have we seen you, Your Grace, nor did Margaret, Lady Tetbery, ever mention you."

It was a lie—a rather bold and inflammatory one, in fact.

The countess, Aunt Hettie's dearest friend and confidante, spoke of her nephew with great praise and always the utmost affection. Her aunt was no doubt making her loyalties known to both the duke and Felicity.

Perhaps her father should have been worried over Hettie's behavior not Mallory's.

The duke visibly paled at the rebuff. "Ah, you see—"

Felicity glanced at Mallory, imploring her to help steer the conversation in another direction. "Nicholas inherited the estate, but he does not deign to visit us often."

"I have many obligations that often keep me away from Tetbery." It was the same excuse her father used to justify his absence. This bill or that bill demanded his attention in London. "But soon, Miss Fields will be joining me in London for the Season, so I am certain you shall see much of both of us."

Actually, that would mean Mallory and her aunt would see *less* of Felicity, as neither journeyed to town, Season or not.

"Really?" Aunt Hettie questioned.

Felicity's aversion to Town mirrored their own, though her reasoning was skewed from Mallory's in a rather significant way.

"Yes—"

"No—"

"Interesting," Hettie countered.

"I'm delighted you are here," the duke said, though his rigid stance spoke to the contrary. "And I do hope you find the estate to your liking."

"Thank you," Hettie huffed. It was the same tone

her aunt used when she deemed her brother was acting the pompous lord, and she need remind him things in the Hughes family would be a great deal different if she had been born male.

Mallory wanted to laugh at the man's obviously awkward posture, and her aunt's thinly veiled contempt for the duke. Instead, she made certain her serene smile beamed, and her manners were above reproach—as her father had demanded.

"It is an honor to meet you, Your Grace." *Especially since you are not my intended arrived unexpectedly after nearly two days of travel*, she added to herself. "I'm Lady Mallory Hughes. Miss Fields has told me much about you."

Namely, setting the man's leg after he fell from a tree—oh, and the frogs in his bed. It is said he cried like a babe each time.

Mallory did not allow her smile to slip as she nodded in the duke's direction.

"All good things, I hope." His tight grin was forced.

Hardly.

"Absolutely," Mallory shared aloud. She kept her gaze trained on the duke for fear she'd burst into laughter if she caught Felicity's eye.

She gave up when Felicity let out a very improper snort.

With the duke appearing satisfied by their introductions, Mallory stepped forward, her welcoming smile returning.

Assessing Felicity, Mallory noted the woman had lost weight, her always tall, thin frame becoming lankier without any added pounds about her hips and bust. It was an issue Mallory's brother was constantly teasing her about—her wide hips, heavy bosom, and legs as sturdy as an aged mare.

Felicity stepped close, and Mallory wrapped her arms about the woman. The embrace was more for Mallory's benefit as she knew Felicity did not see the purpose or gain from human contact. Yes, Felicity had researched the effects of interaction via touching and how it correlated with one's health and mental stability. Her friend had actually written her a fifteen-page exposition on the subject matter the previous year.

The instant they touched, Mallory's vision blurred, and she knew the normally light grey color of her eyes had turned to a deepening, rolling smoke, as if a storm passed through her.

A jolt of scorching heat coursed through her as Mallory blinked several times to clear the vision from her mind.

Peculiar…and intriguing.

She leaned close to Felicity. "So, you shall kiss the handsome duke—"

Felicity stiffened, holding Mallory close for a moment longer to whisper, "I shall die first."

"Suit yourself," Mallory replied with a nod, closing her eyes for a brief moment as Felicity fled her embrace.

Opening her eyes, Mallory saw the duke inspecting her closely. Had he seen the storm rage in her stare when the vision had been upon her? Perhaps, but Wycliffe and his opinion of her were of little concern to Mallory.

What was very concerning was her friend's reaction to the man.

The heat that had coursed through her spoke of Felicity's inner turmoil. She was angry—no, *furious* at something. Likely the duke's announcement his ward would be traveling to London for the Season.

"Shall we go inside, then?" Wycliffe broke the uncomfortable silence, holding his arm out to her.

Mallory silently chastised the man. While she did not seek to be part of society, she adhered very strictly to societal protocols…and society deemed the duke should offer his arm to Aunt Hettie, not Mallory, and most certainly not Felicity—though that would be a sight to see.

Blessedly, Felicity slipped her arm through Mallory's and started for the manor.

"You are greatly vexed, Felicity," Mallory hissed when they were several paces from the carriage, affording them a spot of privacy. "A scorching heat nearly had my knees buckling beneath me."

"We shall not discuss it now," Felicity retorted.

"It is none of your business, my child," Aunt Hettie shushed, making both women jump at her close proximity.

It very much *was* something Mallory need speak to her friend about, yet it could wait a while until the women were left to their own devices and free from Aunt Hettie's hovering.

"Thank you for offering Aunt Hettie and me lodging." Mallory hurried to match Felicity's long strides as they reached the house. "It will only be a day or two—three, at most. Mother wants us returned to Blenheim Park in time for the new year."

"My home—err, the duke's home—is always open to you and your family." Felicity turned a pointed glance on her. "Although, I find it rather startling you are betrothed to a lord you know naught of."

"He will hopefully be far better than the men I do know," Mallory laughed, dispelling the heavy air that had settled about the group. "Now, more importantly, tell me of your project. Last you wrote me, your experiments were progressing with a startling speed and efficiency. Do tell me the duke's arrival will not halt your tests."

"Oh, Mallory." Felicity stepped closer to her but refrained from entwining their arms. "There is so much I must tell you. I am exceedingly close to my goal, but I fear my time is running out."

They stepped over the threshold and into Tetbery Estate, its warm, inviting interior always a calming balm for Mallory. Felicity prattled on and on about her recent discoveries in correlation with her experiments surrounding the Philosopher's Stone, and an elixir to promote immortality. While the matter was of grave importance, and Mallory was anxious to hear all about it, it also afforded her a moment's distraction from what the coming days held for her.

# CHAPTER 2

THE ANCIENT, THICK wooden door slammed solidly in Silas's face, cutting off the miniscule amount of heat that escaped the castle to warm him from the plummeting coastal December air. The envelope in his hand was nearly as dense as the door several inches in front of him.

And it meant nothing.

Addressed to the Earl of Lichfield…the previous Lord Lichfield.

The invitation to attend the wedding of Lady Tamsyn Hambly to Mr. Gryffyn Cardew, and Lady Morgan Hambly to Harold Mort, Viscount Blackwater, on the twenty-fourth day of December, 1811, at Castle Keyvnor had appeared a suitable time as any to make the acquaintance of his mother's family. His funds had dwindled to such a low point—and the Marquess of Blandford had refused to set a wedding date before the new year—that he'd been reduced to doing exactly as Peabody suggested months prior.

He was in Cornwall to throw himself at the mercy of his estranged relations on his mother's side.

The horrid irony that he was still betrothed to Lady

Mallory Hughes was not lost on Silas.

Not even a little bit.

Tucking the embossed invitation into his inner coat pocket, Silas pulled his collar higher to keep the wind from his neck and ears.

His father had not responded to the missive—naturally, because he was dead.

And so, Silas's name had not been added to the guest list, nor a room reserved for his arrival.

The castle was brimming with guests, and his "*fair*" aunt, who "*loved her relations*" was not available to sort out the issue.

Where did that leave Silas?

Admitting defeat. With no other recourse but to return to the tiny, dingy lodgings at the Crown & Anchor in Bocka Morrow, the final room available in town. The finer establishment, The Mermaid's Kiss, had turned him away just as readily as the butler at his aunt's castle.

His aunt, the Countess of Banfield, was in possession of a bloody damned castle!

Silas turned and stepped down from the stoop as the thought sank in.

Sybil would never have agreed to remain in London had she known her relations lived in an ancient castle. There was no doubt the vast rock structure was home to all sorts of ghosts and goblins. Slade would be joining him in Cornwall in a day's time—likely at his besmirched room at the local tavern—due to his recent *troubles* in London and his need to remove himself from certain circles before...

Silas sighed. Now was not the time to ponder the predicament his twin had embroiled himself in.

Silas was in the wilds of Cornwall, preparing to meet his betrothed and resigned to overlook his better judgment to make the acquaintance of his aunt—devoid of proper lodging.

How was he to adhere to Peabody's suggestion and

keep his estranged, pauper status unknown if he were to greet Lady Mallory under such conditions?

At least he could gain a proper bath and pressed shirt at the Crown & Anchor.

The butler had promised to pass word to the countess of his arrival in Bocka Morrow. It would have been wise to bring his bloody calling card to leave with the servant; however, Silas had expected—foolishly—to be greeted by the open arms of family.

Fair and loving be damned.

Worse yet, Slade would arrive shortly.

Silas bloody well hoped the tavern did not sport a gambling room for his twin, or Silas would likely be returning to London on foot, his horse sold to satisfy debts incurred during Slade's stay.

Even more feverishly, Silas prayed his aunt sent word sooner rather than later and summoned him to the castle.

Silas scanned the desolate coastal landscape surrounding Castle Keyvnor. The only break in the monotony of the view was a carriage rolling toward the castle and servants bustling in and out, hurrying to some point beyond the rear of the magnificent structure.

Yet, no sound could be heard beyond the rise and fall of the turbulent ocean waters.

It was this that drew Silas's notice upon arriving in Cornwall: the quiet.

In Paris, the butcher began his work long before sunrise, and the streets were ever brimming with merchants, travelers, and vagabonds. The noise was incessant and comforting in an odd way.

There was nothing comforting about this eerily soundless castle on the cliffs.

Glancing back at the drive, Silas noted that the fast-approaching carriage was only several hundred yards from him now. This was not the way he'd sought to make his appearance at Bocka Morrow. He must be presented to all in a manner above reproach—shrouded in respectability—if he and his siblings had any chance of acceptance among society.

A reputation as the poor, estranged relation was not easily overcome in London.

He swung onto his waiting horse and set off across a barren strip of land toward town—and a tumbler of Scotch.

# CHAPTER 3

MALLORY SAT ACROSS from Aunt Hettie in the formal dining hall as the woman finished her late-morning meal of toast and poached eggs. With Mallory's stomach still churning from her earlier vision, she'd yet to manage even a bite of toast. Aunt Hettie hadn't seemed to notice her aversion to their meal.

Her usual comfort when visiting Tetbery Estate had not presented itself as yet. Since the countess's death, and Felicity's mourning, nothing about the lush, coastal manor gave her the same sense of calm. The servants were not as welcoming—though that could not be their fault—and Felicity was keeping a secret from Mallory. Despite her insistence that they'd speak on the matter at a later time. Mallory was sensible enough to realize it was a ploy to halt her questions about the vision. Certainly, Mallory and her aunt would remain at Tetbery for a couple of days, but when would the time present itself to discuss Felicity's experiments in greater detail?

Ink remained on Mallory's fingertips from when she'd drawn an image from her latest vision on the foolscap provided by Felicity while they huddled in her friend's lab. She hadn't any idea what the symbol meant beyond its connection to the Philosopher's Stone—or so her friend had confirmed. She wished she'd been able to see more, sense more while in Felicity's hidden laboratory that morning; however, it had not come to her. And forcing her visions had never worked except to incite a headache that lasted for days.

Two visions, less than a day apart, and both surrounding her dear friend.

The kiss and the symbol—could they be connected beyond what Mallory pictured when her gift overtook her?

She dabbed her cloth napkin in her water goblet and swiped at her right hand in another vain attempt to remove the blasted ink. Perhaps Felicity could concoct something to cleanse her skin.

The only positive was Mallory had been able to keep the greater nature of her vision to herself. Her aunt would be proud of her for keeping the tidbit to herself. For, truly, Mallory did not seek to change the course of her original vision when she embraced Felicity the prior day, especially if the information might alter Felicity's chance at happiness.

Happiness. It was an odd thing to ponder, yet, as Tressa always spouted, every woman deserved to be happy.

Mallory believed happiness was in her future. If her betrothed, Lord Lichfield, was to bring it into her life, all the better.

"Why are you smiling so, my child?" Her aunt's peeved words cut through Mallory's daze, bringing her back to the present as Hettie wiped a glob of jam from her chin, her narrowed stare all the while focused on her niece. "What has you in such overt cheer?"

Setting her napkin aside, Mallory folded her hands in her lap. "I am always brimming with merriment."

"I assure you, this is different." As Hettie searched Mallory's eyes for some hint of what she was up to,

Mallory did her best to gaze back with less enthusiasm. "You know I can spot a fibber when I see one, correct?"

"Yes, Aunt Hettie." When her aunt turned her attention back to her plate, a sense of accomplishment settled within Mallory. Not that she enjoyed misleading her aunt, but some things were none of her business, including Mallory's knowledge that the duke was, at this very moment, in Felicity's laboratory, and the pair were destined to kiss. Yes, everything had been as it was in her vision: beakers placed and filled with the exact same shade of liquid, Felicity's dress the same black, and the dark, depressing shroud in the room.

With any luck, Mallory would know firsthand the delights of such an embrace.

Though she must needs first make the acquaintance of the gentleman who would claim her first kiss.

"Dreadfully awful coincidence, arriving yesterday to find that pompous duke in residence," Aunt Hettie huffed before spearing another egg. "I cannot think his presence is at all good for Miss Felicity."

Just how horrible it was, her aunt could not know. Even Mallory could not project what was to occur with the duke in residence.

Felicity was up to something—something big if the power of Mallory's vision was anything to go by—and the Duke of Wycliffe's unexpected attendance would muddle everything. Her experimentations had increased in urgency…nearly to the point of desperation.

"You had truly never met the duke before yesterday?" Mallory questioned, keeping her expression as placid as possible.

"Nope, never seen the man."

"Oh, well, Felicity has never spoken kindly of him."

"I think it best we keep a watch on him," Hettie proclaimed, thumping her fist on the table. "He can't be up to anything good. Nothing, I tell you."

"I will do as you wish." Mallory made to stand, a footman appearing to pull her chair back. She smoothed her gown. "Besides, it will keep me occupied until we hear from Lord Lichfield."

Hettie smiled confidently, sensing her nervousness. "The lad will send word as soon as he arrives in Cornwall. The pair of you will meet, you will appear normal, he will be taken in by your classic English beauty, and the union will progress on schedule." Hettie sighed, pausing for a moment. "At least, if that is still what you desire."

It was the unending question her aunt had been asking since her father journeyed to Blenheim Park several months before to discuss the offer of marriage. Though the banns had been read and the announcements posted in all the relevant newspapers, Aunt Hettie continued to prod her over the decision; a choice her aunt hadn't made for herself, and in the end, relegated herself to a life of spinsterhood.

Which was exactly the vision Hettie had for Mallory.

However, Mallory was determined to prove the bloody prophecy wrong.

She had to, there was no other choice except accepting her fate and living a solitary existence alone at Blenheim Park. That was *if* her elder brother allowed her to stay at their family home after their parents passed away.

A throat cleared behind her at the dining hall door, and Mallory's shoulders tensed.

The Tetbery butler stood with his hands clasped behind his back.

His pinched expression did not bode well for what he'd come to announce.

Could it be that the duke meant to rescind Felicity's offer of lodging while they remained in Bocka Morrow?

"What is it?" Aunt Hettie grunted as if the servant,

simply doing what he gained his wage for, was irritating her by his mere attendance. "Out with it!"

The man's eyes widened, and his bewildered stare jotted to Mallory.

"Tolsworth," Mallory attempted to smooth the situation. Peculiar her father was overly worried about Mallory's decorum in social settings—he'd gone so far as to send Hettie with her to Bocka Morrow, after all—but it was her aunt's gruff attitude that might very well jeopardize their success. "Do come in. We were finishing our meal. It was lovely, by the way. Is there something that needs our attention?"

The butler's apprehension intensified. "You"—he glanced at Hettie before addressing Mallory—"you have a guest. He is waiting in the front receiving room off the foyer."

"A guest?"

"Yes, he gave his name as Lord Lichfield," the servant confirmed Mallory's fear.

She glanced down at her ink-stained hand and simple, grey frock. Not how she'd envisioned meeting her future husband; however, there was no need to put the matter off any longer. Once she was satisfied that he was neither a corrupt nor offensive man, she and Aunt Hettie could return to Blenheim Park and await the coming nuptials.

"Then I suppose we shan't keep Lord Lichfield waiting." Mallory notched her chin, hoping the action would infuse her with assurance. Giving in to her trepidation would solve nothing and only lead to increased probing by her aunt. This was what she wanted: a home, a husband, and children of her own. Things that could not be taken from her no matter how peculiar she was or how desperately she avoided society. "Shall we, Aunt Hettie?"

"I suppose." Aunt Hettie hefted herself from her chair, the thing nearly tipping completely backward. If not for the attentive footman, it might have put a hole in the wall. "Though it is rather impolite to appear out of thin air without sending notice."

Mallory had the same opinion; however, she was not as eager to cast a negative light on Lord Lichfield. There were obvious reasons he had arrived unannounced, not following the instructions that he, himself, had outlined in his letter to Mallory's father. Did he deem himself above such things?

A frightening thought, indeed.

"Are you certain you do not wish to freshen up before meeting with Lord Lichfield?" Hettie did her utmost to keep up with Mallory as she departed the dining hall. "Mayhap change your gown or have Miss Felicity's maid re-pin your hair?"

Mallory paused, her aunt colliding with her shoulder at the sudden stop.

She'd dressed that day as she did each morn. The gown she wore had been specifically packed because it highlighted her ample curves and hid her not-so-narrow waist. The ribbon woven through her long, brown curls was of a deep plum that complemented her grey gown. Her shoes were half-boots, sturdy enough for a walk about Tetbery Estate. Except for the ink marring her hand, Mallory appeared as she always did.

Poised. Modest. Genteel.

Everything the daughter of a marquess was raised to be.

That she was anything but poised on the inside was of no consequence, so long as she did her utmost to keep those around her blissfully unaware.

Her talent as an oracle—or a clairvoyant—did not define Mallory. In fact, she was determined to prove her family wrong and live a normal life. That she'd need refrain from touching others—and most objects—did not deter her from believing a normal life could be hers.

"I need not freshen anything. If my simple frock and daily coiffure is not to Lord Lichfield's liking, then imagine if he learned of my *talents*."

"You are not to speak of it," Hettie hissed. "Your father would—"

"My father would die of apoplexy if I embarrassed him in any way," Mallory finished. "Think you I am opposed to this match? I assure you, I do."

Mallory squared her shoulders and marched into the foyer, pausing only to allow the butler to open the parlor door and announce their arrival.

"Lady Henrietta Hughes and Lady Mallory Hughes," Tolsworth proclaimed, giving Mallory a reassuring nod as she swept past him and into the room.

She was vaguely aware of her aunt entering the parlor behind her and the butler pulling the door closed after stating tea would arrive with all due haste; however, Mallory stood rooted to the spot.

She hadn't thought about what Lord Lichfield would look like, nor considered his age when she'd been told of the potential match. He could have been plagued with a hunched back or vertically challenged, but she hadn't questioned that.

The man who stood to greet them was not what she'd envisioned in an arranged marriage.

He was not stout or rounded. He was in possession of all his extremities. And he certainly was not of an age past his prime.

Lord Lichfield did, however, tower over both Mallory and Hettie.

The earl's shoulders were broad enough to pull a cart or roll a boulder up a hill.

And he was handsome. Not in the tradition English sense with a sharp nose, angular jaw, and rigid stance. No, it was far more—yet far less—what her brethren in muslin considered a dashing man.

He had a sophisticated air about him. As if he had seen things, experienced things, Mallory could only guess at.

His clenched jaw, and his clear blue eyes cascading over her, made Mallory wish she'd donned a gown that didn't constrict her breathing in such a manner, as she found it exceedingly difficult to gain a proper breath.

Her stomach fluttered—actually *fluttered* as he gazed upon her.

A single black curl fell over one eye, and he pushed it back before turning his attention to Aunt Hettie.

"Heaven's above," Hettie hissed in her ear.

Mallory stalled from turning to assess her aunt's reaction. While she was fairly skilled with her gifts, her aunt hadn't the need to touch a person or object to gain her visions. The notion of a vision slamming into her at any turn would be overwhelming—and likely a true curse for Mallory. Yet, Hettie had lived with her talents for decades longer than her niece, and her grasp on the power was far superior and less daunting. Or, at least, her aunt proclaimed it to be so.

Lord Lichfield stepped forward, bowing deeply to Hettie. "I am Silas Anson, the Earl of Lichfield." His strong voice reverberated in the room. The earl was certainly blessed with better manners than the Duke of Wycliffe. "Lady Mallory Hughes. It is a pleasure to make your acquaintance, at last."

"I—well—" A cold calm settled over Mallory, despite the heat she'd battled at first seeing the man. When her head spun, and her stomach churned, Mallory reached out for something—anything—to stop her from what was certain to come next. There was little need for the science-minded Felicity to be present to observe and assess what was happening…Mallory was about to faint for the first time in her life. "My lord—"

Where had her aunt gone?

Mallory waved at the empty space beside her where Hettie had been a moment ago.

Nothing said *normal English debutante* like losing consciousness before a handsome lord.

Finally, she grasped on to something, quickly realizing it wasn't *something*, but *someone*.

The lightheaded sensation fled instantly, only to be

replaced by blurred vision as her grey eyes clouded.

Heavens, but there would be no chance of convincing Lord Lichfield that she was nothing more than your usual London lady, which was an odd thought as she was certain she appeared a possessed female.

Lightning coursed under her skin, banishing the chill from a moment before as her focus cleared.

Mallory no longer stood in the Tetbery parlor, but in a garden—a frozen, winter garden—the moon heavy and full overhead. A man stood not far from her, shrouded in the shadows of night, his back to her. Yet, she knew the man, their connection lay deeply within her heart. His black curls were cut short on top, in no danger of falling to block his gaze—which struck her as peculiar. A loud bang sounded close by, and the man fell to his knees before slumping forward into a heap.

A ragged exhale pushed the burning air from her lungs as a strong hand clamped on her arm above her elbow. Twisting, she saw no one at her side in the garden.

She trembled, and her vision began to clear, returning her to the warmth of the present.

Blinking several times, Mallory glanced at her arm where Lord Lichfield held her securely upright, his palm against her bare skin several inches above her glove.

"Mallory—dear child—are you unwell?" An edge of panic laced Aunt Hettie's voice, but she sounded far away. Out of reach. Why?

With a start, Mallory shook herself free of the vision and stared up into Lord Lichfield's anxious face, creased with worry. More surprisingly, her sense of sorrow as she gazed up into his most captivating blue eyes. Her chest ached, and a sense of loss overwhelmed her.

Perhaps her aunt had been correct, and Mallory was destined to live the life of a spinster—for she'd just witnessed the Earl of Lichfield's death.

# CHAPTER 4

SILAS STARED DOWN at the young woman, his focus only leaving her pale face to glance at Lady Henrietta for guidance. When the stoop-shouldered woman gave nothing, appearing as shaken and incapable of words as her ward, Silas sensed he'd need to step in and right the situation. He was obviously to blame for whatever had afflicted his betrothed, though he knew naught what his mere greeting could have caused.

Perhaps this was a precursor to their wedded life? Though he desperately hoped Lady Mallory was not a woman prone to the vapors or flights of fancy. Quite specifically, Silas was worried about Lady Mallory resembling the characteristics of his mother.

Besides, Mr. Peabody would be disappointed to hear he'd ruined all the solicitor's hard work over the previous six months within two minutes' time with his abysmal manners. Not that Silas cared a whit what the incompetent man thought.

"Do have a seat, Lady Mallory." When she shook her arm free from his, Silas opted to guide her to the settee. "I believe the butler said tea would be sent."

Lady Hettie sat next to her ward, and Silas was left

with the choice of either a chair by the hearth—across the room and at the women's backs—or a stool positioned on the opposite side of the low table before their settee.

Eventually, a knock came at the door, and a young maid pushed a cart into the room, stopping at Lady Mallory's elbow.

"That will be all," Lady Hettie blustered, not bothering to turn toward the maid.

With a hesitant smile, the girl dropped into a curtsey and fled the room, returning the door to its closed position. When the latch clicked into place, Silas focused once more on his betrothed.

He noted that even in her frenzied state, she was quite beautiful—in classic Rose style. Long, light brown locks that hung in precise curls. No doubt they would shimmer with golden highlights when exposed to the bright sun, not that England came with many clear, sunny days free of the ever-present cloud cover the country was known for. White, porcelain skin showed a healthy love of the indoors but the hint of freckles across the bridge of her nose exposed a possible secret affection for morning walks. Despite her attractive, poised demeanor it was her eyes that kept him enthralled. He'd seen them cloud over with something akin to a storm rolling in from the sea, enveloping the landscape and casting everything in the darkest shadows. It must have been a trick of the light, perhaps the dimming of a candle that had made her grey eyes darken moments before.

Lady Mallory continued to struggle with inhaling a satisfying breath. Her chaperone whispered in her ear as she rubbed her back.

His piqued interest would not remain unnoticed for long. Moving to the short stool, Silas lowered himself, all the while praying the delicate contraption held his weight. Blessedly, the thing did not crumble or even so much as creak. As if a switch were flipped, Lady Mallory focused on him, her eyes going from cloudy to clear within an instant as she reached out to the tea service. A perfectly composed smile settled on her heart-shaped, full lips—though she could not hide the increased weight on her shoulders.

"Tea, my lord?" Her posture was recumbent, and her voice even with hints of a soft melody.

Silas wagered the woman had an exceptional singing voice.

"My lord?" Lady Mallory's brow furrowed.

"Yes, please," Silas sputtered. Anything that did not use up his remaining coin was exceedingly welcome. "Tea would be very welcome."

Lady Hettie reclined on the settee and glared at him, not hiding her scrutiny. Though he supposed her age and social standing as the marquess's sister precluded her from a few social niceties.

"Lady Henrietta Hughes," Silas coaxed, making certain his voice remained calm and low, relaxed. "I offer my thanks for accompanying Lady Mallory to Bocka Morrow. As she had an aversion to London, and I was journeying to Cornwall for my cousins' weddings, this was very beneficial for all."

"We reside in Northern Cornwall," Lady Hettie grunted. "'Twas not as far as London, or this body I've been cursed with would not have made the distance, I assure you."

Silas glanced at Lady Mallory, but the woman seemed oblivious to the tête-à-tête between her chaperone and him as she prepared three cups of steaming tea. Not once did she pause to question if he preferred cream, sugar, or honey; yet, she combined the perfect amount of cream and sugar for Silas's liking. It was how his mother took her tea each day, and it had grown on the countess's three children.

"You are one of three siblings?" Lady Hettie questioned as if reading his mind.

Unsettling.

Lady Mallory handed her chaperone a delicate teacup and saucer, painted with perfect roses, before leaning across the table to Silas's cup.

"Thank you." He glanced down into the swirling tea, giving himself a moment to think before the impending questions about his lineage were asked. It was the way of things in England—it was not a man's integrity or worth, but his family connections that meant everything. "Yes, I was blessed with a younger brother and sister, Slade—or Sladeston—and Sybil."

"I have an elder brother, as well. Adam," Lady Mallory offered, bringing her cup to her lips. "He mainly resides in London and only returns home for holidays. We are not close."

She pressed her lips tightly.

He wanted to smile, offer a measure of reassurance. Speaking of family, no matter the closeness, was a difficult thing. He'd often found himself giving too much information, or none at all.

"While I am very close to my siblings, it is because it is only the three of us." Silas would not mention that Slade had had an unfortunate run-in with Lady Mallory's brother in London only a few short weeks back. Thankfully, word had not gotten back to the marquess, thus affecting his and Mallory's betrothal. "And you, Lady Mallory, are you enjoying your stay at Tetbery Estate?"

Silas was no stranger to uncomfortable, awkward conversations. It seemed every interaction with his mother, the Countess of Lichfield, ended in some odd utterance or proclamation. Once, for the brief period she'd fancied herself a sculptor, Mary Louisa had demanded her children refer to her as Charioteer. Many years later, the countess had taken to local superstitions and insisted the trio walk backward whenever in her presence.

Shaking his head, Silas realized he'd missed whatever Lady Mallory had been saying.

"...Miss Felicity Fields and her servants, as well."

"Very good." At least he hoped that was the appropriate response.

"Do give your family our felicitations on their upcoming nuptials."

He certainly would, as soon as his aunt acknowledged his existence—if that ever came to pass.

"I've only seen Castle Keyvnor from afar," she shared, a new light coming into her pale grey eyes. "The place appears menacing yet fascinating at the same time. I have heard—from both Miss Felicity and Tressa—that spirits roam within its vast corridors."

Spirits? Silas hoped his betrothed did not believe in the fallacies of ghouls, ghosts, witches, and curses.

It was not as if Silas could speak of any hauntings within the castle walls. He hadn't been permitted beyond the front stoop.

"I only arrived in Bocka Morrow yesterday. I have yet to explore the castle in any regard." It was not a lie. He had reached Cornwall the day before, and since the butler had turned him away, he'd been unable to sightsee on the property. At her crestfallen look, Silas continued, "However, when I do find the time for exploration, I will certainly keep my eyes and ears open for anything of an occult nature."

His answer seemed to satisfy her, and her smile returned.

The woman would unquestionably do for his countess: demure and cultured, if a bit shy. And agreeable.

Yet, something hinted that there was more to the woman. He watched her as she took a deep drink of her tea, her eyes closing briefly as she enjoyed the flavor—or possibly the soothing heat—of the liquid.

Silas only need avoid shackling himself to a woman as flighty and fickle as his mother. Prone to emotional tirades and undeniable shifts in demeanor, his mother, while loved and cherished by all her children, had not been their provider. After fleeing England—and the control of his father—Silas, as a young child, envisioned a life of adventure full of marvelous, grand places and people. Instead, his mother had been content to stow her children in a one-room flat in a seedy part of Paris while she explored her artistic endeavors.

Years later, Silas had pondered the true reasoning behind his mother's flight from England. Had there been a man she thought herself in love with? Perhaps pursued a promise of a future together. When he'd asked, his mother had waved off his questions as she did everything. Her children's hunger, their education, a sprained ankle in need of a doctor's care—his questions were no more important to her than those.

Meaning, there was aught that interested his mother beyond her own self-interests.

Silas would not wed a woman like the countess.

"Tell me, Lady Mallory, what hobbies have you?" he asked, setting his cup aside but keeping his intense stare on her. Even in her youth, it was said that his mother had such tendencies, and perhaps his betrothed would hint at similar interests, thus allowing him to avoid years of heartache before they commenced.

Her back stiffened, and Lady Hettie let loose an unladylike snort.

Did women in England not spend their free time in pursuit of hobbies?

Truly, what hobby would he deem normal and not in keeping with a woman in possession of a capricious mind?

Surely, needlepoint was acceptable. Even watercolors were a tolerable pastime. Though, a musical talent would be preferable to a love of oils or sculpting.

At this point, it would only further tarnish his family name if he walked away from their betrothal at such a late juncture. The banns had been read, the match announced in both London and his local parish, and he'd even found his mother's simple gold wedding band in his father's desk at Ditchley Hall.

When both women remained silent, Silas feared he'd overstepped some invisible boundary between cordial social call and intrusive interloper.

He pushed to his feet, the stool thankfully remaining upright after his sudden action.

"I think it is time I return to the castle," he mumbled. "It has been a pleasure making your acquaintance, Lady Mallory. I look forward to our joining in the spring." There, simple enough as goodbyes went. "Lady Henrietta, also lovely meeting you. I do believe you and my sister will take to one another quickly."

Neither woman moved from their seats on the settee as he bowed. In fact, Lady Hettie hadn't so much as taken a sip from her cup, though she'd brought it to her lips several times.

"You are staying at the castle?" she inquired, though her focus was on the cup in her hands.

"Yes, until after my cousins' weddings. Then I will return to my estate, or mayhap accompany my brother to London." It seemed important he answer the woman's question, though he owed her no response. "Safe travels to you and Lady Henrietta. I look forward to your arrival at Ditchley in the spring."

For a man who prided himself on knowing what was what, Silas could not determine with any certainty if he was or was not looking forward to Lady Mallory's arrival at Ditchley. What he could say with all certainty was that despite this short time speaking with her, he did not have any greater understanding of the woman before him, or why she'd need resort to a union with a stranger coordinated by her father's solicitor. She appeared like every other young woman he'd met since arriving in England.

"Good day, Lord Lichfield." Lady Henrietta pushed to her feet, her hunched shoulders making it impossible for her to reach her full height, though he suspected it was shorter than her niece's. "Mallory and I wish you well. My brother, the marquess, and Mallory's mother look forward to traveling to Hampshire when the time comes."

"My family will be honored to meet the Marquess and Marchioness of Blandford."

The door to the salon opened as if the servant had been waiting with his ear pressed to the wood in wait.

"I will show you out, my lord." The butler nodded toward the foyer, and Silas had little choice but to follow.

Their meeting had done little to ease his trepidation regarding their coming nuptials.

# CHAPTER 5

THE DOOR CLOSED with a thump, causing Mallory
to nearly leap from the settee, a splash of tea spilling
over the rim of her cup, marring her cream glove. The
liquid should have scalded her skin, even with the
protective layer of fabric, but the droplets were only
room temperature.

How long had she, her aunt, and Lord Lichfield sat
in the Tetbery receiving room?

Glancing at the window, the dark blue drapes
pinned back to allow light into the room, Mallory noted
the sun had progressed high into the sky. The day was
clear and would be unseasonably warm. Why were icy-
cold tendrils of dread racing through her?

Lord Lichfield was naught more than a stranger, a
man her father had selected for her, without so much as
meeting him if she'd heard the earl correctly.

She had no ties to him. She owed him nothing. In
turn, he was not indebted to her.

It should not matter what her visions showed for
his future.

"My child," her aunt said, taking the cup from her
tight grasp. "What is it? What did you see?"

Mallory swallowed. How could she tell anyone—even her most dear aunt—she'd lose her intended, likely before they were even wed?

Her vision had shown a winter-kissed garden with a moon glowing from above, lighting the blossomless shrubbery sufficiently enough for Mallory to take in the scene.

A shiver coursed down her spine, and her aunt leaned into her line of sight that was still focused on the window.

"I have an awful pounding in my head." Shaking off her aunt's hold, Mallory stood, struggling to keep the room from blurring about her. "I think I will retire to rest. The journey from Blenheim Park must have me more exhausted than I'd realized. Do give my best to Felicity if you see her."

"You do not look well—"

Mallory forced a weak smile. "I promise it is only my head. A spot of rest will have me feeling much improved."

Neither woman believed Mallory's lie, and to be honest, she wasn't concerned with disappointing her aunt. If anyone knew the hardships of their gift, it was Aunt Hettie. For many years, Mallory had watched her aunt fight through her visions and seek refuge in her solitary existence. She could not deny her niece the same recourse, especially if she were to keep her gifts hidden from her betrothed.

In that moment, Mallory realized that Aunt Hettie's fate, and the loneliness it brought, was not something she hoped to live with in her own life.

"I will attend you at supper." Her voice did not crack on the words. "We can speak of Lord Lichfield at that time."

"You worry me, my child." The woman's brow knitted as she stared up from under her heavily hooded lids, attempting to straighten her stooped back. "Tell me what you saw, and I can—"

"I saw nothing...of import," she added to assuage the guilt that surged at her continued deceit. "Until our meal."

Mallory leaned down, placing a quick kiss to her aunt's plump cheek before she fled the room. She kept her pace sedate and even until she reached the main stairs. The front door was firmly shut, Lord Lichfield gone and the butler disappeared to parts unknown, freeing Mallory to expel a bit of her apprehension as she took the steps two at a time until she was racing down the deserted hall to her assigned room.

The door closed without a sound.

The click of the latch falling into place seemed to open Mallory's airways, blessedly allowing her to draw in a deep breath. Concentrating on the rise and fall of her chest, constricted by her corset and tight bodice, Mallory's heart slowed its frantic pace. Her headache receded, and she clenched and unclenched her fists at her sides.

She hadn't been affected by a vision in this manner since she'd seen her father's end in a particularly vivid revelation when she was but eight years old. The startling occurrence had rocked Mallory to her soul. No child should see their parent perish, even if only in a vision. Though the same could be said for a father learning of his impending death from his offspring.

That was the day her brother, Adam, had labeled Mallory a curse, a hex, and a blemish on her family. A lump formed in her throat at the memory. It was the day she'd been sent to Blenheim Park, separated from her father, mum, and brother, to live with her addlebrained Aunt Hettie.

However, as it turned out, Aunt Hettie was far from senseless. For if she were crazy, that meant Mallory was also afflicted with the crux of insanity.

Mallory did not feel dull or senseless.

In fact, her visions were usually clear and precise.

All too vivid and accurate for her family's liking.

Her breathing returned to normal at last, and she moved to the window thinking to push it open and allow in a cool breeze. Perhaps it would also clear her mind and give her some idea of what was expected of her. Rarely did she keep her visions to herself when they so evidently impacted another.

But death…that was not an omen she easily shared.

She'd only been presented with such life-changing visions on two previous occasions: her father's death, and that of Felicity's guardian, the countess. She'd spoken of it to her father and had been sent away. Mallory had been wise enough to keep her knowledge of the countess's sudden passing from Felicity, and she'd felt immeasurable guilt since. Felicity, had she known the end was near, could have taken better advantage of her time, perhaps planned for her future in a more sensible manner.

It was not Mallory's choice to keep her vision from Felicity, but the countess's. She'd been right, though. Her dear friend was burdened by many deaths in her life, and the countess hadn't seen the need to speak of it to her ward.

Aunt Hettie had agreed, and Mallory had promised to remain silent on the matter.

That had been during their visit the year before.

Mallory sighed and released the cord holding her window shut and the winter cold out. The sky was as it had been earlier, without a cloud. The trees in the distance swayed from the wind coming off the ocean. In the distance, Castle Keyvnor stood high and proud along the cliffs, ancient, mysterious, but also, in an odd way, welcoming. Could it be the ghosts—and other less human entities—drawing her to them? Did her special gifts align her with others of her kind?

Perhaps Aunt Hettie and her companionship was not enough to soothe her ragged soul.

Male voices drifted up to her second-floor window, and Mallory leaned forward, expecting to see the

Tetbery Estate's groundskeeper or a groom, but she quickly leaned back inside when she glimpsed Lord Lichfield below. Inching out to peer over the window ledge again, Mallory saw he spoke with the duke. Both appeared at ease, as if they'd met before and conversed about something, but their voices were not loud enough for her to discern what they spoke of.

It was not impossible Lord Lichfield was acquainted with the Duke of Wycliffe.

England wasn't an overly large country, as it were, and London could be downright stifling with people, or so Aunt Hettie had proclaimed numerous times over the years.

She watched as both men chuckled, Lichfield throwing his head back, allowing his mirth to travel up to Mallory above. She couldn't help but think her betrothed was not one quick to laughter. When their chuckles halted, Lichfield ran his hand through his wayward, onyx curls. She wondered if his hair would be of silky softness or coarse to her touch.

Her stomach fluttered at the thought of running her fingers through a man's hair—that it was her soon-to-be husband only caused her pulse to race once more. Mallory was uncertain what she'd expected to happen when they met. Seeing his death was as startling as the realization that she found him pleasing to the eye. Had she ever thought a man handsome before?

Perhaps, there had been a groom or footman at Blenheim Park she'd fancied herself smitten with, but rarely did she make the acquaintance of a proper lord.

The Duke of Wycliffe was a decent enough man, yet she hadn't imagined her fingers in his light brown hair.

The sound of horse hooves signaled that Lord Lichfield's mount had been brought round, and he would soon depart for the castle and his family.

Mallory risked being spotted as she moved ever closer to peer down at the men.

With the swiftness of a man used to horsemanship, Lord Lichfield mounted his horse and waved farewell to the duke.

However, instead of going toward the castle, he maneuvered his horse in the opposite direction. But that could not be. He'd stood before her and claimed he needed to return to the castle.

Mallory glanced back in the direction of the sea cliffs as unease settled over her.

Why had he lied about his intended destination?

They were not wed, only betrothed.

Until they joined as husband and wife, the earl had little need to share anything of his daily comings and goings with her. In fact, even after they wed, it was not her business to question him on such matters. As her father was wont to say, men—lords especially—were challenged with duties and responsibilities mere females could not possibly understand.

Certainly, Mallory did not believe a word of it.

She stood at the window and kept her focus trained on Lord Lichfield as he rode at a leisurely pace away from Tetbery Estate.

Her mother, the marchioness, might be resigned to such old-fashioned ways of thinking, but Mallory was not.

The earl had lied to her. Looked her directly in the eye and told a falsehood. But to what end?

Was this the stepping-stone to what would eventually cause his downfall?

Her aunt was correct: Mallory had no obligation to inform Lord Lichfield about her vision; however, she did have a duty to keep the man alive, at least until after they'd wed. If she remained unwed, the prophecy of her aunt's vision would be undeniable.

Mallory would forever more remain a spinster.

No home to call hers.

No family of her own.

Forever at her brother's mercy.

Without another thought, she collected her cloak from the wardrobe and rushed from her room, down the servant's stairs, and out the back door by the kitchens to the stables beyond. Blessed was she that her dear friends, Felicity and Tressa, had spent so many years showing her ways to get around Tetbery without being noticed. Even if her aunt or a servant caught her, Mallory had no intention of slowing down.

She needed to follow Lord Lichfield and discover exactly why he'd lied to her…and what else he hid from her.

She crossed the garden quickly, the early-afternoon wind catching her curls and pulling them out behind her as she ran. By the time she reached the stables—and the warmth within—she'd slipped her arms into her cloak and was fastening the buttons.

"Lady Mallory," a young stable hand stuttered, obviously taken aback by her appearance. "M'lady, what can I do ye for?"

"I need a horse."

The boy only stood, gawking at her as if she'd asked for an elephant to be readied.

"You do have a horse I can ride, do you not?" she prodded. "Miss Felicity told me—"

At the mention of his mistress, the lad jumped into action. "O'course. Where ye be need'n ta go?"

"I thought I'd see about purchasing a Christmastide gift for my mother," Mallory said. Not a complete fib as she'd thought to stop in one of the larger towns on the way to her family estate to collect a few gifts for her family. "I know the village is near, but I rarely visited town during my stays in Bocka Morrow."

"It be that way, m'lady." He nodded in the direction Lord Lichfield had ridden. It was just as Mallory guessed. "'Bout a ten-minute ride, it be. I can prepare the carriage for ye."

"No, that is not necessary." And would garner far more attention than Mallory wanted. Her aunt would not allow her to follow Lord Lichfield. "Just a horse will do."

If the stable hand had any qualms about sending a lady into the Cornwall countryside—alone—he did not speak of it. Mallory silently thanked Felicity and Tressa for their independent ways as the servants were likely used to women going about unchaperoned.

In quick order, a light brown mare was led into the main room of the stables, and a block set down to assist her onto the sidesaddle. Again, she counted her blessings that Aunt Hettie approved of women on horseback. She was proficient atop a horse and would have little trouble making it to town. She need only catch up to the earl.

Losing sight of him during his ride would only make matters difficult.

Properly mounted, Mallory turned to the stable hand below.

"Sir." She smiled, hoping her charms would be enough.

"Yes, m'lady?" he asked readily.

"I won't be gone long. If you'd be so kind as to keep mention of my departure to yourself, I would be ever so grateful." When the lad's stare darkened in question, she continued, "You see, I am going to town to buy a gift for my aunt, as well, and I desperately wish to surprise her."

"I see," he whispered back as if they shared a grand secret. "I won't be breath'n so much as a word ta no one, m'lady."

"Very good," she said, taking the reins from him. "I shall return as quickly as possible."

The lad nodded, and Mallory nudged at the mare, pulling at the reins until they were out of the stables and starting across the meadow—not toward the castle but the seaside town of Bocka Morrow.

# CHAPTER 6

BOCKA MORROW'S TINY tavern was nestled in the heart of the fishing district close to the docks with its sullied white paint peeling from the siding, and the good cheers and lighthearted conversations floating outside to where Silas stood waiting for the groom to take his horse. The salty sea breeze of the waterfront pushed the clouds toward the far horizon and away from Tetbery Estate. And within the dim confines of the local public house, The Crown & Anchor, Silas suspected he'd find what he sought—at least for the moment.

Everything about the lowly tavern screamed for Silas to beware.

But what was a man to do when he was in a foreign fishing village, a long way from home, and in need of lodging?

The Mermaid's Kiss had been full to brimming with the *ton* coming from far and wide to witness his cousins'—Lady Tamsyn and Lady Morgan—wed, and he'd been turned away outright. Which was likely preferable, as his coin would gain him much more at The Crown & Anchor anyways.

He only hoped it wasn't a knife in his back or bed

mites under his skin.

A lad ran forth from the side of the tavern, his hair tussled and in need of a trim, his shirt with more holes than the cheese Silas had dined on the previous evening, and no boots to speak of. The elements alone in Bocka Morrow were enough to have Silas thanking the heavens above he'd brought his thick wool coat as opposed to only his finely tailored jackets. The boy was certain to catch his death and be in need of a physician before long.

"Welcome back, m'lord," the groom called with a toothy grin. "Old Havers be give'n away a right fine gin in the tavern."

Silas wanted to ask what the boy knew of "right fine gin"—but the question went unspoken in favor of a far more vital one. "Where are your boots and coat, lad?"

The groom's eyes widened before taking in Silas's attire from head to toe, his stare riveted on his gleaming Hessians. "Life ain't all 'bout fancy boots and toff coats, m'lord."

"That is true, but one cannot discover what life is all about when they are taken low by influenza." He stopped short of adding, "my boy." When the lad said nothing in return but took the reins from Silas, he dug into his pocket and extracted two shillings—not an exorbitant amount of money by any means, but enough to find a pair of boots—and tossed them to the boy. He did not miss a beat as he swiped them from the air.

"What this be for?" he called, opening his palm to see the shine of the coins. "Two bobs…"

"Boots, lad," Silas called, starting for the tavern door before the boy could argue at the offer. "It is a bounty for taking good care of my horse because I would not have the guilt on my head if he stepped on your toe and cut it clean off. Find a pair of sturdy boots as soon as you unsaddle my mount."

Silas doubted the boy would use the shillings

properly, though he could not give up all hope at a satisfactory outcome for the groom. He was young and agile—and if he managed to starve off frostbite from his extremities, he could certainly be more than a mere stable hand at a seedy waterfront tavern.

With a sigh, Silas entered the crowded public room; the smells of unwashed bodies, stale ale, and fish greeted him more welcomingly than Lady Mallory and her aunt. Perhaps he was better suited to this lowly tavern then his rightful place at Castle Keyvnor.

Bloody hell, it had been embarrassing to hide the fact that he was not residing at the castle during his stay in Bocka Morrow—nor even at The Mermaid's Kiss— from Lady Mallory. Silas was uncertain what bothered him more, lying to his intended or actually having to stay at the god-awful waterfront public house when his *family* lived so near.

Finding a place at the high bar, he took a seat on an empty stool and nodded to the barkeep, who immediately poured him an ale without asking what he wanted. The glass arrived smudged and unclean, but the ale was adequate.

His day hadn't gone as planned. Not at all.

His first meeting with Lady Mallory had been disastrous, to say the least. The girl had nearly fainted at the sight of him, and her aunt had stared daggers the entire visit. His betrothed was comely, in an innocent maiden sort of way, demure, and reserved. Besides her moment of lightheadedness that had nearly called for salts, she seemed relatively ordinary. Certainly, her cloudy, grey eyes were worrisome, but nothing else caused his hair to stand on end.

Now, she could return to her family home, and he could go about his business.

At the moment, Silas waited for *his* business to summon him. He had no doubt his aunt would send for him at some point, if for no other reason than pure curiosity. Until that happened—and he prayed it was before Slade arrived in Bocka Morrow—Silas would prioritize his needs: meal, drink, and sleep.

Unfortunately, with the added coin given to the groom, his funds were thinner than before.

Glancing about the room, Silas envied a group of men sitting around a low wooden table, its surface scarred but ladened with fresh, crusty bread, poached fish, and cheeses. His stomach rebelled at the sight. For now, ale in a filthy mug would have to do.

He must needs save his coin for his evening meal and a proper bath before journeying to the castle to meet his long-lost family.

The warm ale slid easily down his throat to appease his stomach, and Silas attempted to block out the carousing and laughter of the tavern's other occupants. He wondered if anyone in Bocka Morrow actually earned a decent living as they were all solidly in their cups at such an early hour of the day.

At the thought, Silas drained his glass and signaled for another.

If he were going to crash and burn—with both his betrothed and his mother's family—he might as well be deep in his cups to soften the impact.

The form in which the impact would come was unknown; however, there was no doubt he'd survive it. Lady Mallory could discover he was a pauper without familial ties in England. Or, debatably worse, his aunt would give him the cut direct and banish him from Castle Keyvnor. Either way, the scandalous information would make the gossip rags, and the Marquess of Blandford would call off the betrothal—as he had every right to do. Whether Silas wanted to admit it or not, he and Mr. Peabody were deceiving the marquess, even if only by lies of omission.

In the end, Silas would have no option but to return to his estate, financial ruin continuing to loom over him, and without proper familial ties.

Slade's mounting gaming debts to worry over only

increasing his need to escape the impact of failure.

There was always Paris, he reminded himself.

Yet, fleeing back to France came with a completely different set of complications—namely, his mother.

Something nudged his shoulder, causing ale to splash over the rim of his glass and splatter the bar top.

"My apologies," Silas mumbled to the barkeep as the man wiped away the mess.

He didn't glance over his shoulder to see who'd disturbed his brooding, but the distraction was welcome. His mind had been heading toward dangerous territory.

Very dangerous territory, indeed.

"Come on now, sweet meat," a gruff voice crowed. "Ye come sit on Pa's lap."

Laughter flared throughout the room; some deep and hearty while others far more hesitant with apprehension.

"No." The female reply was spiked with discomfort but held a measure of finality. "I be here ta work, not sit on ye lap."

"Oh, ye be work'n if ye sit, I promise ye that, wench."

The man's word started another round of chuckles at Silas's back, and he closed his eyes against the urge to step in. This was not his town, and not his fight. The barmaid could take care of herself—women in her profession were resilient and held a measure of cunning most men never gained. If that failed, the barkeep would put a stop to the harassment.

If word spread that he was causing problems, sticking his nose where it didn't belong in town, the Countess of Banfield would have all the more reason to turn him away. He needed to remember his plight was not only to help his lot in life but also that of his siblings. Sybil needed proper sponsorship when she made her debut next Season, and Slade, he needed to be shackled to a solid stone wall in the basement of the castle. Because if he kept up with the mounting gaming debts, Silas would need more connections in London than even the countess could provide to keep his twin safe once his debts were called in.

"I said no!"

Again, something knocked his shoulder, giving Silas no option but to assess what was transpiring behind him.

The instant he turned, he saw a brawny, bearded man, recently off a fishing vessel judging by his smell, slipping a hand into the serving maid's bodice. No one jumped to her aid. In fact, the barkeep turned the other way, and the tavern patrons were suddenly very interested in their cups and meals.

He should have entered The Crown & Anchor and sought his room after returning from Tetbery Estate; however, proper conduct was proper conduct, no matter where you lived or who your relations were.

No man had the right to set hands on a woman if she said no.

End of story.

Having raised his younger sister—and in many ways, his own mother—Silas adamantly refused to support the mistreatment of women, be it his sister or a perfect stranger. Barmaid or princess. Orange seller or opera singer.

Silas pushed from his stool and stepped before the man, separating the pair. If the woman was smart, she'd slip from the room and be well hidden until after Silas disposed of the offending man.

"Get outta me way, you toff." The man's chest puffed in an attempt to intimidate Silas. "Mind ye own lot."

Silas shook his head, feigning regret, and placed his hand on the aggressor's shoulder. "I'm afraid that won't be possible."

With a firm squeeze on the man's collarbone, Silas guided him toward the door.

"Let me go, ye brute."

"One would categorize you as the brute, sir." The maid scurried out of the common room, and Silas pushed the man out the door and into the early afternoon sun. "I think it best you seek out your home and be done at The Crown & Anchor for the day."

The man appeared ready to argue, but his lips clamped shut, causing the vein in his forehead to throb. If he threw a punch in Silas's direction, it would surely hurt like the dickens.

The villager, clearly a seaman from the stains on his trousers, would not be so foolish as to assault a stranger.

Silas blocked the door to the tavern, crossing his arms over his chest, and waited for the man to depart either on foot or horseback. However, he only stood staring at Silas, his fists clenching and unclenching at this sides as his face turned molten red.

"Do not be a buffoon—"

The fist came out of nowhere. One moment, Silas watched the thing clenched at the man's side, and the next, it landed solidly in Silas's gut. His only saving grace was that the short distance separating him and his opponent was not wide enough for the man to gain any momentum for his punch. The second swing came at Silas's head, and he ducked with a swiftness he hadn't known he was capable of. The man's fist traveled harmlessly through the air.

Unbelievable. What had transpired in his life over the past six months that Silas went from the museums and art galleries of Paris to the waterfront taverns in the wilds of Cornwall—not to mention having a drunken fool coming at him with wide-eyed rage?

Speaking of wide-eyed, raging fools, the man stumbled back when his fist connected with only air but came back quickly, teetering forward as he lunged at Silas once more.

Silas's thick, woolen coat only hampered his movements as he sidestepped the man but swung around quickly to prevent him from entering the tavern again.

A crowd gathered just inside the public house as the patrons pushed close for a view of the skirmish.

*Bloody hell.* Everyone at Castle Keyvnor and Tetbery Estate would likely hear of the tavern brawl before the day ended.

Silas needed to put an end to things before they went any further and someone was gravely injured. It would not do to arrive at the castle with a shiner or, worse yet, be made to seek out a physician due to broken ribs or a fractured arm.

The next round came with the agility of a man half his size and a decade younger as a fist collided with Silas's shoulder; however, he was able to block the man's right hook aimed at Silas's chin.

This only angered the seaman further, his mouth thinning into a grim line as his brain worked through his next move.

Silas could fairly see the wheel turning as he assessed his opponent's weak areas. Unfortunately, he did not know that Silas had saved every spare penny to pay for sparring lessons in his youth: bare-knuckle boxing, fencing, and wrestling. If Silas had wanted to cause a bigger commotion by taking the man down, he would have done so before fists flew in his direction.

The man's move was clear, the telegraph so evident on his face it was a wonder he'd survived any past brawls.

He made to lunge at Silas again, spreading his arms wide and preparing to grab him about the chest, but the man halted before he pushed off and crumpled to the ground at Silas's feet. A boulder the size of an ale pitcher hit Silas's ankle and rolled into the tavern behind him.

What in the blazes?

Someone had stepped in and put an end to the scuffle.

Silas should have welcomed the assistance; however, it was unwarranted and unnecessary. As if he needed someone to step in and rescue him.

He stepped out of the tavern's doorway and turned to the interloper, a rebuff on the tip of his tongue.

What he saw had Silas staggering back a step, his eyes widening in shock, surprise, and confusion as his pulse slowed to normal.

His mouth opened and closed several times as he searched his mind for the right thing to say. Hell, at this point, he'd be satisfied with gibberish nonsense.

Before him stood Lady Mallory Hughes, her wayward curls hanging haphazardly about her shoulders, her cloak's buttons undone, her cheeks reddened from either the brisk December air or the excitement, and dear heavens above, Silas could not look away from her.

With lips pursed and arms still raised above her head from throwing the rock that had connected with the seaman's head, Lady Mallory was anything but the poised, demure London debutante he'd met an hour before.

Her grey eyes fairly sizzled with unbridled heat as they took him in, scrutinizing his arms, legs, chest, and face—for injuries?

Certainly not.

Confident that he was whole and unharmed, Lady Mallory lowered her arms to her sides and took a deep, ragged breath, her chest straining against her bodice.

She was strong, self-assured, and robust. There was no spark of madness in her eyes as he noticed them darkening in the afternoon sunshine.

"What are you doing here?" he demanded.

"I could ask the same of you, my lord," she retorted without hesitation, her stare narrowing on him as if challenging him to lie.

Not that Silas had any reason to lie.

"You should be at Tetbery Estate, not gallivanting about the Cornwall countryside." He stepped forward, hoping to steer her away from the man at his feet who was beginning to stir and the crowd gazing on from the tavern. "You could have been seriously harmed."

Pulling from his grasp, she huffed and hurried ahead of him before rounding and pinning him with a hardened stare. "It is you, Lord Lichfield, who was in jeopardy. And feel free to offer your thanks for my rescuing of you."

"You, rescue me?" No one rescued him. It was Silas who took care of everyone around him. And it appeared that would extend to his betrothed, as well. He laughed, "Don't be addlebrained, Lady Mallory. It is you who will be harmed if your escapades become known."

Her eyes flared with irritation, and she crossed her arms over her still heaving bosom. "If my escapades are made known to whom?"

"Anyone," he retorted. "Your reputation would be tarnished."

"And you would be free to find fault with our betrothal?"

Find fault with their betrothal?

Silas's mind whirled in an attempt to keep up with her words. "I have no intention of crying off. I committed, papers have been signed, and the banns read in both my parish and published in the London papers."

"It is only your name on a piece of parchment that has bound you to me?"

"Are you mad, woman?" Silas knew the error of his words the moment they crossed his lips.

Lady Mallory's nostrils flared with fury, and her lips pulled back, baring her clenched teeth.

When she took a step toward him, Silas backed up, out of shock or self-preservation, he was uncertain.

When her eyes narrowed on him, one hand landing on her hip as the other rose, she said, her words clipped, "You—think—me—mad?" She poked her finger into his chest with each venomous syllable.

In his entire life—as challenging and unpredictable

as it had been thus far—Silas realized he'd never known true fear until he looked into the slate-grey eyes of his betrothed.

She was both terrifying and utterly captivating.

It was as if he were being led to his very own reckoning,

And he waited with bated breath to discover his fate.

# CHAPTER 7

MALLORY GLARED AT the scoundrel, her soon-to-be husband if her father had anything to say about it, daring Lichfield to repeat his previous folly and utter the word *mad* again. Her blood boiled, and she suspected her cheeks were aflame despite the chill in the air.

Space. Distance. Time.

To think. To reconcile. To breathe.

*That* was what Mallory needed.

Instead, she took another step forward, and he answered by retreating.

It was the word whispered behind raised hands in her household: mad, insane, lunatic, crazed, frenzied…

Each spoken to wound her or Aunt Hettie.

Spoken behind closed doors by her father, uttered directly to her face by Adam, and whispered behind her back by the Blandford servants.

Years of pent-up hurt and anger surrounded the use of that one, simple word—or any of its derivatives.

And Lord Lichfield was unaware of her gift and therefore associating the spiteful comment to other portions of her person.

It was he who was in the wrong in this situation,

and it had naught to do with her. She hadn't so much as breathed a word to anyone about her visions. Though one had overtaken her earlier, Mallory had recovered quickly and even fooled Aunt Hettie into thinking it hadn't happened.

Damnation, but she was doing everything she'd promised her father. She was putting on a show much like any actress upon the stage—normal, poised, and proper.

Not unconventional, unsuitable…rejected by those who should cherish her most.

"Lady Mallory." His pleading tone darkened her resentment as he attempted to reach out to her. Sidestepping his reach, she could not allow him to touch her and risk another vision. "I spoke out of turn, I did not mean to insinuate that you lack any—"

"Unfortunately, you did," she seethed, her fury rising again at his obvious effort to justify his words. "Lord Lichfield, you lied to me."

"I lied to you?" he asked, startled by the switch in topic.

"Yes, you told me you were on your way to Castle Keyvnor when you left Tetbery, but here you are, at the public tavern, imbibing spirits long before the hour is proper." A sudden cold breeze pushed her curls over her shoulder, and she clamped her jaw tight to keep her teeth from chattering. Perhaps it was Lord Lichfield who was unsuitable, not her. "Am I to wed a drunkard, my lord?"

A single, perfectly arched black brow shot up at her demand. "It is not against any law for a man to enter a tavern to quench his thirst."

"Very true. However, my concern is not with the drinking itself, unless you tend to imbibe in excess, but with the fact that *you* lied to *me* and in front of my aunt." Mallory supposed she might well be overreacting a tad and her grievance was not solely with his falsehood. "Furthermore, I wish to know if you have a penchant for carousing and physical altercations."

Her finger still jabbed at his chest—his solid, muscular, broad chest—as she spoke, and Mallory dropped it to her side. Thankfully, his chest was not bare, and her gloves were solidly in place. There was a small likelihood someone from the castle had witnessed their argument and recognized them.

Perhaps Lord Lichfield had a point: her behavior was a bit erratic. Surely not mad, but when she'd spotted the man as big as an ox pummel the earl in the ribs and then nearly bash him again, she'd had to put an end to it all. The boulder sitting near the tavern entrance had been an adequate weapon, especially as neither fighter had seen the blow coming.

If her betrothed were to perish, it would not occur with Mallory standing helplessly by.

Unbeknownst to this man, he'd not only committed to a betrothal and a marriage to her, but he was her lifeline, her chance at a future above and beyond being the spinster daughter of a marquess. He was to give her a family and a home of her own. A place where Mallory could be herself and fear nothing.

Felicity had that at Tetbery, and bloody hell if Mallory did not long for her own sanctuary.

The man before her was her ticket out of her father's—and brother's—control.

And he would damn well follow through with things.

Lord Lichfield exhaled in a labored burst, his shoulders falling. The arrogant set of his chin seemed to relax, as well. "No, Lady Mallory, I am not a drunkard nor prone to lying." He pinched the bridge of his nose, but Mallory remained silent, waiting for him to continue. "I was hungry and in need of a drink. Meeting one's betrothed for the first time can be downright taxing, and the castle is overrun with guests, servants, and the like, all preparing for the weddings and ball to follow. I did not wish to be underfoot or a nuisance to anyone. So, instead of returning to Keyvnor, I came into Bocka Morrow for a meal and a pint of ale."

"Yet, that led to fisticuffs with—"

"That was in no way fisticuffs," he said, cutting her off. "That offensive man thought himself justified in harassing a barmaid. I was merely showing him the error of his ways by escorting him out of the tavern."

"You could have been seriously injured," Mallory said, releasing the breath she held as all fight left her. If this man would go to such lengths to honor a maid he did not know, how far would he go to support his own wife?

"That was a possibility; however, the potential injury to the barmaid at the rascal's hands was far greater, do you not agree?"

"It…I…well…" Had she judged him wrong? Had she been too harsh with him? The fact of the matter was that they were to be wed in a few short months, and Mallory needed to know the quality of the man she'd be tied to for all her days. If he were cruel and callous, prone to drinking, or quick to temper, Mallory would fear ever allowing him to learn of her gifts. "I suppose your actions were very gallant, my lord."

"Silas, my given name is Silas." He ran his fingers through his hair, the curls landing precisely in place. "I suppose if you've bashed a man senseless to save my hide it is only right you call me Silas."

*Silas.* A unique name, indeed.

Very fitting.

Odd, but she'd never once thought to know the man beyond his title or address. Certainly, he'd given his name when he introduced himself earlier. It would be peculiar if she continued to address him in such a formal manner—even in their private chambers.

"Am I wrong to assume you came to town without benefit of a chaperone?"

"You would not be incorrect," she mumbled, embarrassed for the first time at her rash decision to follow him. "Though I can assure you, no one will notice my absence."

He turned away from her and paced a few feet before swinging back around to face her.

"Did you bring a horse, or did you make it here on foot?"

She glanced over his shoulder to where the young lad held the reins of the Tetbery mare she'd borrowed. "A horse."

How had she gone from scared that he'd be injured to furious at his hurtful word to feeling like a recalcitrant child who needed forgiveness?

"Let us get you back to Tetbery Estate before anyone misses you," he sighed.

"No one will miss me, and I can find my own way back."

"While I am certain both of those statements are true, I cannot allow you to go unattended." He held up one finger to stop her protest before it had even formed on her tongue. "It is not for your sake but mine. I will worry incessantly if I do not witness you arriving safely at Tetbery with my own eyes."

She'd be lying if she didn't admit that a jolt of approval coursed through her at his proclamation. Something fluttered in her chest.

Lord Lichfield, Silas, was not a cruel or crass man.

Perhaps they would suit well.

# CHAPTER 8

MALLORY SAT IN her rear-facing seat, her hands twisting and knotting in her skirt as their carriage made the short jaunt to Castle Keyvnor. She'd wallowed in remorse all night, her guilt finally getting the best of her when the day dawned clear and bright.

The carriage hit a deep rut and sprang back up as the well-maintained Wycliffe conveyance gained a bit of speed. The desolate seaside terrain was nothing like the lush greenery surrounding her family home in Launceston. Though still in Cornwall, her estate did not have the unrelenting winds and salty ocean air constantly battering the land.

Aunt Hettie groaned on the seat across from her and readjusted her position from where she'd slumped low.

"I told you I was perfectly capable of calling on Lord Lichfield at the castle without you," Mallory replied, keeping her irritation from entering her tone. "It is only a ten-minute carriage ride away from Tetbery. You could have practically seen me arrive from your bedchamber window."

Her aunt shook her head with a frown. "Not

proper, not proper at all, a girl tramping about Cornwall unchaperoned. That Banfield family would have a right good laugh at the lot of us."

Mallory had been correct in her words to Lord Lichfield—Silas—the day before. She'd slipped back into Tetbery without anyone the wiser. When she'd joined Felicity and her aunt for their evening meal, her dear friend had offered a powder to be taken with table wine to diminish the ache in her head. Mallory had nearly ruined her own excuse when she questioned what Felicity spoke of, but she'd recovered with swiftness, thanked her friend, and taken the awful mixture.

She may not have had a headache before, but the mere disgust of the powdery substance almost incited one.

"You do not agree with my match to the earl?" Mallory asked, already sensing her aunt's response would be to the affirmative. "He is a kind enough man."

Aunt Hettie snorted, crossing her arms over her heavy chest. "You met him for no more than an hour's time. You cannot know if he is kind—or much else. He hardly spoke of anything of a personal nature." Hettie glared at Mallory across the carriage. "Plus, he was raised in France. An English lord, raised in France. What will people think?"

At her aunt's questioning stare, Mallory remained quiet. Never, in all the years she'd lived with her aunt, had Mallory ever witnessed Hettie giving a single care for what people thought of her or her choices in life. It had to be a ploy to convince Mallory the man was unsuitable because her aunt knew Mallory cared greatly about what others thought of her.

Mallory would not fall into Hettie's trap.

Nor could she admit that she did, in fact, know beyond a reasonable doubt that Silas was an honorable man.

Which was exactly the reason they were headed toward Castle Keyvnor.

She needed to apologize for not trusting him, for accusing him of intentionally lying to her, to assure him she was resigned to their match. More than resigned, as it were, but content with it.

If she and Hettie left Bocka Morrow to return to her family estate, Silas could determine she was unfit to be his countess and send word to her father to discuss the matter. He'd said he had no intention of crying off, but with her less than appropriate behavior the day before, she would not blame him for running. He likely thought himself tied to a hellion, which was certainly not the case. She need only convince him of that.

Once she apologized for her erratic comportment and confirmed her commitment to their betrothal and coming marriage, she could return home knowing she'd made the best impression possible—under the circumstances.

Their carriage hit a large bump, and Mallory grasped hold of the side to keep from tumbling off her seat. The road between Tetbery Estate and Keyvnor was not a heavily traveled one. Felicity—nor her guardian, the countess—ever mentioned visiting the castle.

With the Duke of Wycliffe now taking his rightful place at Tetbery, that might very well change.

The carriage rolled to a stop outside the fortress.

Mallory looked out her window at the intimidating fortification and had to crane her neck to see all the way to the imposing towers above. They stood so tall, they shrouded the carriage in shadows. The stronghold was massive, boasting a moat and battlements—much like the castles so popular many years before. Mallory could envision invaders setting their sights on Keyvnor, prepared to loot and plunder its hidden bounties. Men would be at the ready on the parapets above to defend their home and their families against the raiders.

The carriage door swung open, and the footman lowered the steps, reaching in to assist Aunt Hettie down.

Mallory glanced at her when she made no move to take the servant's proffered hand. Hettie's face had drained of color until she appeared nearly green with sickness and her hands visibly trembled. With her eyes clamped shut, Mallory could not ascertain if a vision had struck her.

She slipped to her knees on the carriage floor without thought of the damage to her skirts and took her aunt's shaking hands into her own. Rubbing them between her palms, warm and moist with nerves, she attempted to banish the chill from her aunt's fingers. Yet, Hettie did not acknowledge her, nor was she calmed by her niece's presence.

Releasing her aunt's hands, Mallory cupped Hettie's face to still her quivering chin and bid her to open her eyes.

When Hettie only tried to pull from Mallory's hold, she relented. The woman's gift was too powerful and all-consuming when it struck.

"I will have the driver return you to Tetbery with all due haste," Mallory whispered. Her heart ached for her dear aunt, her own chest feeling constricted by some unknown force that held Hettie captive, as well. "Close the door!"

"No, no, my child," Hettie mumbled. "Go forth and see Lord Lichfield. Say what needs said, and we shall return home after. I will not enter Castle Keyvnor—I cannot."

"Is it safe for me?" Mallory was familiar with her aunt's aversion to entering certain domains or so much as walking across random paths. While Mallory's visions overtook her when she touched people or objects, her aunt's gift was much more prolific than that—she sensed things without touch. A mere smell could send her aunt reeling as an image invaded, clouding not only her irises but also her mind. Hettie nodded, keeping her eyes closed. "Then I will send you and the carriage back to Tetbery and have it return to collect me."

"I—I—" Hettie struggled to gain strength. "I will wait here—in the drive—for you. You shan't be long."

"Are you certain?" It seemed inconceivable to leave Hettie in the drive in such a state.

"Yes, my child." Hettie straightened her shoulders, her eyes fluttering open to show no storm within their depths. "I will remain here and rest."

Still, Mallory was hesitant to leave her. "I can take you home and return with Felicity—or possibly Tressa—on the morrow."

Hettie shook her head with such force, her cheeks wobbled and her eyes glazed over. "You will go now." The older woman pushed Mallory away and waved to the waiting servant. "Do assistant my niece down."

With one last, lingering look at her aunt, Mallory collected her handbag and departed the carriage. She knew better than to think her aunt would relent and allow Mallory to see her back to the estate.

Her cloak billowed around her in the brisk, bitter cold. Tugging at her hood, she stared up at the castle, her view uninhibited by the bevels in the windowpanes of the carriage. It struck her as odd that anyone actually lived in such a place. Its ancient facade and imposing size were daunting, even to Mallory as a visitor.

"Shall I announce your arrival, my lady?" The Tetbery footman stood at her side, staring up in awe at the castle.

"No, thank you," she said with a reassuring smile. "I can announce myself."

At least, she hoped she could find her voice after knocking on the door that appeared large enough to drive a horse and carriage through.

Mallory ran her moist palms down the front of her cloak and lifted her chin, ready to walk up the steps of the castle as if she belonged. In fact, she did. She was betrothed to the Countess of Banfield's nephew, after all. Soon, she would be family, and might well visit often.

The thought did nothing to assuage her nerves.

The sound of shouting drifted on the breeze. Servants and finely dressed men and woman bustled about in the gardens close to the castle. Mallory stood, riveted, watching people come and go from a side terrace in the winter garden. The rolling greenland, so close to the sea, was breathtaking—and also very familiar.

Impossible.

Clearing her throat and slipping her hand through the drawstring on her handbag, Mallory started for the door. She did not want to keep Hettie waiting, especially if the coals grew cold and the interior of the carriage turned frigid.

Hettie's words sprang to mind…"*You shan't be long.*"

It hadn't been a request for her to hurry, but more of an undisputable truth. Had Aunt Hettie's vision been directly connected to Mallory? Glancing over her shoulder, she expected to see her aunt in the carriage window, but the woman was not pressed to the glass. She reclined in her seat—all but dozing with her eyes shut and her mouth gaping.

Perhaps she was only fatigued.

Starting up the steps, the door opened before she raised her hand to knock.

"May I help you, my lady?" The servant's brow rose in question as he stood in the doorway, blocking her view of the foyer beyond.

"Lady Mallory Hughes, here to call on Lord Lichfield—the Earl of Lichfield," she said, stumbling over her words. *Drat.* She needn't say Lord Lichfield and the earl. She pasted a confident smile on her lips despite the unease that coursed through her at the servant's pulled brow and blank expression. "Is he receiving at this time?"

With a flourish and a deep bow, he gestured for her to enter. "This way, Lady Mallory."

She proceeded him into the foyer and waited for him to lead her to where she would wait. Her pulse raced at the thought of seeing Silas once more. He was certainly the most handsome man of her acquaintance. Surely many debutantes would be envious of her match.

At no point had she ever been in possession of something so grand it was worth envious stares from others; however, her betrothed was very worth the jealousy.

"This way."

The butler started off down a corridor, and Mallory heard voices carrying through the drafty castle from all directions. Silas had not been wrong when he said Keyvnor was bursting with guests. As they passed a room, the open door gave Mallory a view of several young women gathered close as they worked on their needlepoint. The next hall gave her a clear view of a couple slipping into another room and closing the door behind them.

Mallory had never been one to seek the company of a large gathering; however, she'd relish the opportunity to know what the women spoke of as they plied their needles to task.

"Please wait within. My la—Lord Lichfield will be summoned."

Mallory entered a delicately feminine sitting room. With drapes, wall coverings, and furniture of varying shades of peach, the area did not seem like any place Lord Lichfield would dare enter. She smiled to herself at the thought of him perched on the low lounge before the hearth, his weight certainly too much for the furniture to bear.

She pushed back her hood and unfastened the top button of her cloak.

The rest of the sitting room was outfitted in similarly fragile pieces: a writing desk, table and chairs, and a harpsichord nestled in the corner with a short stool.

"The Countess of Banfield," the servant's voice thundered through the room, though he spoke no louder than when he'd greeted her at the door. "Your guest, Lady Mallory Hughes."

Mallory whipped around to face the stately mistress of Castle Keyvnor.

There must be some mistake. She was not here to call on the formidable Countess of Banfield.

Her mouth gaped open and then snapped shut at the woman's frown.

"Lady Banfield." Mallory dropped into a curtsey, pausing in her deep pose for a few seconds longer than necessary to collect her thoughts. Where was Lord Lichfield? Would he be joining them? Why had the servant summoned the countess? "It is an honor to make your acquaintance."

Mallory straightened with a serene smile as she called upon her many years of decorum training in the schoolroom.

None of those lessons prepared her for facing the woman before her.

"I would say the same, but I haven't the faintest notion who you are or what you are doing in my home." The countess looked down her long, beakish nose at Mallory, pinning her with a stare that was both intense and lackluster at the same time. "Well, girl?"

It took her a moment realize the countess truly had no clue who she was. "Well, I am Lady Mallory—"

"I know that much from my butler," the lady snapped, waving her hand toward the servant, who immediately backed from the room and closed the door. "What. Are. You. Doing. At. My. Castle?"

Her slow, deliberate words had a blush rising up Mallory's neck. Thankfully, her cloak hid the worst of her embarrassment. "I am here to call on my betrothed, Lord Lichfield."

"Impossible," she huffed. "Lord Lichfield is my brother-in-law and safely wed to my sister, Mary

Louisa."

"I assure you, my lady, I am betrothed to Lord Lichfield, Silas Anson." Mallory paused to take a deep breath. "While I did not travel with the betrothal agreement, we are, indeed, set to wed early next year."

"Silas, you say?" The woman's tone softened immediately, and she took the few steps to the lounge, lowering herself to sit and then gesturing for Mallory to do the same on the chair opposite her. "Silas. I have not seen him since he was a lad of six or seven before Mary Louisa took…"

Her words trailed off as if she'd said too much; however, Mallory thought she hadn't spoken nearly enough.

"You must be mistaken. Lord Lichfield is staying at Keyvnor and attending the weddings of his cousins— your daughters, I presume." From the woman's severe look, it would have been wise for Mallory to keep her assumptions to herself. "I am here from Launceston, Northern Cornwall, and staying at the Duke of Wycliffe's estate, Tetbery." It felt like a betrayal to Felicity to refer to Tetbery as Wycliffe's property, but there was no way around it. "I am there with my aunt, Lady Henrietta Hughes. Lord Lichfield paid a social visit to Tetbery yesterday."

"My dear, dear, *dear* girl." The countess clucked her tongue with each address. "I am sorry to say you have been misinformed. My nephew is not staying at the castle, and neither was he invited to the wedding. Although, if something happened to his father, I suppose the invite would, socially speaking, be transferred to the new earl, which would indeed be Silas. But I can assure you, I have not seen him. You say he is in Bocka Morrow?"

"Yes, but—"

"If the lad is in the area, rest assured I will locate him." The countess stood suddenly, and Mallory followed suit. "This is not good, not good at all."

"Why ever not?" Mallory asked.

"Because if my nephew has claimed the title, that means two things: my brother-in-law passed away without anyone sending word, and my sister, Lady Lichfield, has no doubt returned to England at long last."

Silas had mentioned nothing about his mother's return to England, only that his siblings had accompanied him from France. "I am afraid I can speak to neither."

The countess stepped forward, reaching for Mallory's hands and clasping them tightly. "Regardless, this is wonderful news. Wonderful news, indeed." Lady Banfield paused as if realizing she still held Mallory. "You and your aunt, Lady Henrietta, must come to the wedding...and the Yule ball to follow."

As Mallory was ushered to the front door and unceremoniously deposited on the stoop, her waiting carriage in the drive, she remembered nodding at the countess, but if that simple gesture meant that she'd accepted the invitation, Mallory was uncertain.

Glancing at the sky above, she noted the sun had not moved at all.

Aunt Hettie was correct. She hadn't been long inside, but much had changed in the short time she was.

# CHAPTER 9

SILAS'S MIND REELED with such ferocity he feared falling from his horse. It was as if he had been caught up in a strong wind and could not right his person as strong gale gusts continued to blow him to and fro with no end in sight. He still sat motionless at the end of the drive to Castle Keyvnor where the main road split in several directions. One would take him closer to Tetbery Estate, one to Bocka Morrow and the open sea beyond, and the last…London.

Everything screamed for him to take the fastest route back to London, away from his *family* and Lady Mallory.

When the servant had arrived at The Crown & Anchor the evening before, unmistakably garbed in Banfield livery colors, with a hastily jotted note from the countess, Silas had agreed readily to meet with her at the allotted day and time. It was his main reason for being in Cornwall, after all. It hadn't even irked him that his aunt hadn't given him an option for the time or place. He would have attended her in the dark of night in a tavern, if she'd requested it.

Perhaps he should have been more leery about the

information she had to impart.

Yet, it hadn't dawned on Silas that he'd been summoned based on anything other than his visit when he first arrived in Bocka Morrow.

He'd regretted his decision the moment his aunt entered the room and wrapped him in an embrace so firm, he thought she'd broken one of his ribs—his chest still a bit sore from the altercation at the tavern. Once they'd been seated, and she began talking at great length and with much vehemence, Silas had allowed the words to wash over him. He'd listened to her speak of the letters and money she'd sent to Paris, the many trips she and his mother's other siblings had made across the Channel in vain attempts to bring Mary Louisa and her children back to England, and the countess's condolences at Silas's father's passing.

If he believed any of it, he'd need to accept all of her words as truth.

It was a daunting thought. Silas had spent most of his life cursing his family, his mother included, for the cruel nature of his childhood. He'd blamed his father for not coming to bring them home. He'd despised his mother's family for abandoning them. And he'd resented his mother for being such a fickle, delicate woman.

When the countess had asked after Silas's mother, he'd seen a tear in the woman's eye when he spoke of his mother's refusal to leave Paris; however, a spark had entered her hard stare at the news that Slade and Sybil were in England once more.

If his entire foundation hadn't been ripped from beneath him, his aunt's mention of his betrothal to Lady Mallory Hughes had surely done it. The woman had professed her remorse over not hearing of his father's death but she'd known of his betrothal. It had quickly come to light that his intended had paid a visit to Keyvnor to meet with him but had learned he'd lied about his status as a guest at the castle.

The cold wind swept inland off the sea at his back, chilling him to the bone through his coat, reminding him that he still stood at a crossroads, one of both the literal and emotional kind. Silas only hoped no one watched him from the castle.

Silas had no urge to return to his dank, musty room at the tavern. Nor was he prepared to admit defeat and return to London.

That only left Tetbery Estate...and Lady Mallory.

When the countess had initially spoken of Lady Mallory's visit, there had been an intense pounding in his ears. He'd withdrawn from the conversation with his aunt, but quickly realized it was his fault it was all happening.

He'd no right to be angry with his betrothed.

Silas had lied to her. He'd been given the opportunity to clear his conscience and admit his wrongs, but he'd continued with the charade.

But there was little doubt left that his aunt had shared all his secrets.

Lady Mallory would know of his estranged status with his family, his lodging at the tavern, and certainly, the dire financial state of the Lichfield earldom.

It would be she—and her father—who called off the betrothal, as what man would wed his only daughter to such a man? And what proper lady would seek to tie herself to a family in ruins?

He'd thought Lady Mallory, with her aunt in tow, would have already departed Cornwall for their home in Launceston in order to arrive before Christmastide morning.

Again, he'd been wrong to assume anything.

Obviously, she remained at Tetbery Estate.

Silas tilted his head back, his eyes closing, and took a deep, fortifying breath. It seemed his obligations were never-ending: his siblings, his estate, his family, and now, Lady Mallory.

There was only one direction open to him, and it

led back to his betrothed.

Lady Mallory deserved an explanation, and Silas was the only person to give it. If she could see past his deceptions and accept his apology, there may still be hope for them.

Oddly, Silas was perturbed to realize he actually longed for Mallory to forgive him. The woman was unlike any he'd met before. Silas's mother was indecisive, scatterbrained, and undependable. His fear of Lady Mallory being, in any way, like the present Lady Lichfield had been ungrounded.

Silas kicked his horse into action with a backward glance at the castle.

His aunt had made amends—or at least she'd made an effort—and had invited him and Slade to join them for the Yule ball. She went so far as to pledge her support for Sybil during her coming Season.

But first, Silas had to make things right with Mallory.

No longer was it essential he wed for the societal acceptance a connection to the marquess would give him and his siblings. Everything he'd dreaded coming to pass over the last several months since Mr. Peabody proposed his marriage to Mallory to remedy some of the Lichfield quandary was not as overwhelmingly frightening as it had been before his arrival in Bocka Morrow.

The sun shone brightly upon his face, and the wind receded as Silas rode toward Tetbery Estate—and the woman with the captivating grey eyes.

# CHAPTER 10

MALLORY STEPPED OUT the door and into the bright sun, bringing her arm up to shield her eyes from the harsh glare as her vision adjusted. Pushing the door shut, she leaned against the rough surface as the scents from the garden invaded her senses. The smell of hellebore roses, or the Christmas roses as Aunt Hettie fondly called them, drifted on the light breeze as the sun crested above in the cloudless sky. The outdoors normally brought with it a feeling of peace and rightness—being surrounded by so many lovely, growing things.

However, after her morning in Felicity's lab, it only brought to mind that which was gone forever, never to return, never to draw breath, never to live again.

Her dear friend had taken to the notion of using alchemy to bring her guardian, Lady Tetbery, back to life. It was a fool's errand. Anyone with an ounce of sense would know working with ancient tomes, the mythical Philosopher's Stone, and combining oddly scented chemicals would not return the countess to life. She was gone, deceased all these months. It was no wonder Mallory could not put the visions of strange symbols from her mind.

In the end, Felicity would fail, Lady Tetbery would never walk the grounds of her Cornwall estate again, and Mallory would need to be there for her dear friend when she grieved the loss of her guardian all over again.

Mallory pushed away from the door leading down into Felicity's lab, determined not to dwell on the pain destined to come for her friend.

She hadn't even time to speak with Felicity about what she'd learned at Castle Keyvnor the previous day. How insignificant was it that Mallory sought her friend's ear to speak of her troubles with her betrothed, while Felicity had lost her guardian, was about to lose the only home she'd ever known, and the man responsible was darkening the halls of Tetbery at every turn?

Walking across the small, fenced-in garden, Mallory lightly caressed the pale pink petals of a winter rose, her touch soft enough not to disturb the precious blossom. How uncomplicated the life of a hellebore rose was, coming into full bloom during the dreariest months before wilting as the warm springtime heat bore down on them…only to return once the weather turned cold again. She envied the blossom's ability to know its place, the proper time to show its beauty, and when to hide from the world.

Perhaps it would have been best for Mallory to stay at her family estate until the time for her wedding arrived. She would not have known the trivial way her father had bartered his only daughter—to a man he'd not so much as met. Lord Lichfield would have had no reason to deceive her either. Yet, that had been a decision he'd knowingly made. Did he think her so petty and lacking in compassion that the state of his relationship with his family would matter?

From what the countess shared, Silas was in no way responsible for the separation between his mother and her family. Neither did that estrangement cast a cloud of scandal in Mallory's eye. Silas hadn't proven ungentlemanly in any way since their meeting. In fact, he'd shown himself to be the opposite.

Besides, hadn't she been keeping her own secrets?

And what she kept hidden from him was in many ways far more scandalous than an estranged family.

Releasing the blossom and moving away from the foliage that disguised the door, Mallory sagged on the low stone wall facing the long drive that ended at the main road. Her aunt was in a hurry to depart Tetbery Estate and return to their home. Mallory was not so certain they should leave now, especially with the countess having invited her to celebrate the holiday at Keyvnor. No one awaited their return to Blenheim Park as her father rarely journeyed to the country, and her brother would likely spend his time with his latest mistress in town.

She hesitated to return to the main house, lingering ever longer in the lush, concealed garden. Solitude had been hard to come by since her arrival at Tetbery, and Mallory had refrained from claiming another headache.

Maybe she could remain hidden in the garden for a while longer.

Gazing out over the vast land surrounding the estate, Mallory wondered what it would be like to have her own home, land, and life. Free from her aunt's watchful eye, and away from the whispered proclamations that she'd been cursed. It was likely that if her betrothal to Silas were called off, she'd never know such independence. A part of her sensed that Silas would not treat her as her father and brother did. He would not tread lightly in her presence, nor eschew physical contact with her.

Yet, another part of her—possibly a larger part— was well aware that she did not know the man well. He could be lying about other things—more important aspects of his life than had been discovered.

Truly, his deception had harmed no one, least of all her. There were many things she was embarrassed to admit about her life, why would Silas be any different? Because he was a man? An earl, no less?

Mallory raised her hand to shield her eyes as a lone man on horseback came into view, a large cloud of dust following him. The Duke of Wycliffe must be returning from town or the castle. As the rider drew closer, Mallory raised her hand and waved. Despite Felicity and Aunt Hettie's feelings about the duke, Mallory thought him an agreeable man and a kind host.

His appearance brought to mind the vision Mallory had seen upon greeting Felicity. While her friend had yet to speak of it at any length, Mallory knew the two had kissed—in Felicity's lab, no less.

The rider took note of her and angled his mount away from the front entrance and toward the small garden pressed close to the side of the manor.

Her stomach sank when the man pulled his horse to a stop and dismounted.

It was not the duke, but Silas.

And she could not deny his look of displeasure.

"My lord," she called, swallowing past the lump that'd settled in her throat. "I did not expect to see you again."

His brow rose, and she knew he'd misinterpreted her greeting.

"What I meant was that I hadn't expected to see you again at Tetbery Estate."

"Because you thought to visit me at Keyvnor again?" He did not pause to see her reaction but quickly tied his reins to a branch that hung low by the garden wall before flipping the latch on the gate and entering the garden. "I am sorry if I disappointed you."

Disappoint? Mallory stared at him to see if his words were meant to be a jest, but he turned serious eyes on her. "Pardon, my lord?"

"I have come from the castle. My aunt, the countess, spoke of your visit." He paced around the garden, avoiding her stare as he walked in a seemingly aimless pattern.

"I did not mean to cause any trouble—"

"It is not your fault." He finally turned toward her and placed his arm to his chest. "It is I who lied, Lady Mallory, and for that, I am eternally remorseful."

Mallory blinked several times. *He* was apologizing to *her?*

"May I ask why you deceived me?" The question was risky. He could refuse to answer and depart. "If it is not too forward of me."

He watched her as if determining whether she was worth the added effort of an explanation. "My mother raised us in Paris, as you know, but something you may not know, is to do that, she fled England under cover of night and never spoke to my father again." He ran his fingers through the curls atop his head, a gesture that was not so much born out of frustration as she'd first suspected, but unease.

He was preparing to share something with her he hadn't told anyone—or at least not recently. The tension in his shoulders lent evidence to that, as well as the hard set of his jaw.

If he could share a bit of himself, then Mallory could share something more, as well.

Certainly not everything about her gift, but maybe enough to keep him vigilant, concerned for his safety.

His lips moved to speak, but a loud rumble shook the ground beneath them. Thrown off balance, Mallory stumbled toward Silas, her arms pin-wheeling when her boot became tangled in her skirts. She was going to fall, face first into the mossy garden ground, or worse, hit her head on the stone wall.

Mallory clamped her eyes shut tightly. She could not bear to see what came next.

One minute, there was nothing but frigid December air surrounding her, and the next…her head was swimming. Though not due to being knocked senseless, as she was still upright. Despite her eyes remaining closed, she knew she was not on the ground. However, she was pressed against something solid

Lifting her hands, Mallory ran her fingers across a smoothly muscled chest and continued upward to graze taut, broad shoulders.

Lord Lichfield's.

Mallory titled up her chin ever so slightly, suspecting if she opened her eyes—which she certainly was not prepared to do—she'd stare directly up into intense blue pools.

Her lips parted, an apology on the tip of her tongue, but the words never made it to her throat as Silas's warm exhale cascaded against her cheek, banishing any cold that lingered within her.

He was so close. There was no need to open her eyes to see that his mouth was only an inch from hers. She could all but feel him.

"Thank yo—"

Her appreciation for his quick movements to steady her was cut off when his lips captured hers. Blessedly smooth, strong lips. Warm. Eager. Moist.

This…this physical connection wasn't anything she'd allowed herself before. There was too much risk.

As if on cue, she opened her eyes, and they immediately began to cloud. The edges of her sight blurred at the same time she raised her hands from Silas's shoulders to cup his face.

*Damnation.* If she were going to be cursed with a vision at the exact moment of her first kiss, she would at least enjoy the feeling of him for a brief instant. Even through her gloves, she knew his skin was smooth and firm across his angled jaw.

His mouth danced across hers.

Mallory's entire body trembled, and his sinewy arms came to wrap around her waist, catching her before her knees collapsed beneath her, bringing their bodies ever closer.

The vision was upon her. Her head began to spin,

and nothing before her remained in focus. His lips caressed hers, the warmth of his arms held her tightly to his chest, and his woodsy scent filled her other senses.

Space…she needed distance to collect her thoughts, banish whatever horrid vision was struggling to capture her, and—

The late-morning air filled with the acidic smell of fire.

Mallory released her hold on his face and stepped back at the same moment his arms fell to his sides.

She pivoted quickly, her heart racing from their embrace as she blinked several times to clear her sight. Smoke billowed through the cracks of the partially hidden door to Felicity's laboratory.

"Felicity!" Her dear friend had been working in her lab when Mallory left her to seek a few private moments in the garden. Felicity had been combining one liquid element with another in her quest to bring back the countess. "We must help her."

Her knees, trembling when she'd been in Silas's hold, strengthened as she raced toward the door.

# CHAPTER 11

SILAS FOLLOWED CLOSELY on Lady Mallory's heels when she took off toward the smoke—and a red slatted door, the paint chipped off at the bottom to reveal the aged wood behind thick strands of ivy. It hadn't dawned on him that anything was amiss— besides his forwardness in stealing a kiss from his betrothed—until she pulled back, and he was able to take the lead and draw his first deep breath since capturing her in his arms.

Smoke, thick and dark, clouded his vision and clogged his lungs as he ripped the door open and proceeded up the steep, narrow steps as hard packed dirt turned to stone. The smoke thinned when he traveled farther up the stairwell as great billows of it escaped downward. There was no need to glance over his shoulder and risk tripping up a step; he could sense Lady Mallory's presence at his back, though she moved a bit slower as she climbed. When she'd disentangled herself from his embrace, he'd noted the familiar darkening of her eyes, much as they had on their first meeting.

Yet, there was no time to think about the peculiar

way the light grey orbs had turned a tumultuous charcoal, nor could he allow his attraction to slow him down.

Someone was in trouble, and he must needs make certain they were away from the fire causing all the smoke around them.

When he reached the top step and pushed into the room, halting, Lady Mallory bumped into his back but quickly steadied herself on the railing.

"Where was she?" Silas squinted as he inspected the hazy room, attempting to locate the source of the fire—or, more importantly, Miss Felicity, especially if she were injured and needed help getting out. "Are you certain she was up here?"

The room was lined with workbenches stacked high with large tomes, several lying open as if Miss Felicity had been reading them recently. Another long, low table with an empty stool was arranged with several glass bottles of varying sizes and shapes. On yet another, jars lined the surface holding god knows what sort of foreign things. The smoke came from a stout glass container filled with a bluish-green liquid. The fog rolled over the top in dense but waning clouds and then floated upward.

"She was there," Mallory said, pointing over his shoulder at the far workbench, but Miss Felicity was nowhere in sight.

Mallory pushed past him and swiftly moved about the room, searching for her friend.

The urge to pull her from the lab to safety was nearly overwhelming.

"The room is empty, Lady Mallory," he called, taking her arm to halt her search. "I have no idea what caused the smoke, but we should not dawdle here. The haze could harm our lungs."

She pulled from his grasp and turned large, rounded eyes on him. "But—but—she was here not long ago."

"But she is not now." The smoke was clearing quickly, giving Silas a clear view of the entire room. It was not overly large, and there was nowhere Miss Felicity could lurk. "What is all this?"

With one last glance about the work area, the tension appeared to flee Lady Mallory, and her shoulders sagged. Silas was going through a similar change, the immediate danger and terror subsiding and allowing their present circumstances to invade the moment.

He'd kissed her.

He'd come to Tetbery Estate to make amends with Lady Mallory, to throw himself at her mercy. Instead, he'd kissed her. Anyone could have seen them. It hardly signified anything if someone had. They were properly betrothed, and their wedding date set for as soon as the ground thawed. Their embrace wasn't scandalously compromising.

Why then did he sense he'd complicated things between them instead of making them better?

Their kiss—more accurately, his response and the way she'd melted against him—proved they suited in the physical sense.

Mallory ran her fingers along one of the workbenches and paused to read one of the open books. "Felicity conducts vital experiments here."

"She is a scientist?" His short time in England had not offered any information on Miss Felicity Fields. No one he'd met with spoke of the woman.

"Of sorts."

"How can one be a scientist of sorts?"

"She's set her mind to exploring the Philosopher's Stone and the mythological chemical compound for immortality."

If Mallory had any opinions regarding her friend's activities, she made no mention of it. There was no judgment or disapproval in her tone. Silas wasn't certain he'd take the same stance if one of his friends—not that he had any besides his siblings—spoke of such a harebrained idea as immortality.

He folded his arms across his chest as the final remnants of smoke cleared, and Mallory continued her slow walk about the room. With her attention focused elsewhere, Silas was free to truly take in the woman. With her dark brown tresses and petite height, she did not appear a woman who gained notice when she entered a room; however, Silas was unable to take his eyes off her. The natural sway of her rounded hips, the curve of her backside she could not hide even beneath a cloak, and the graceful poise she always seemed in command of.

"Immortality is something of make believe, is it not?" he asked, glancing away before his attraction became more apparent. When she only shrugged, he continued. "Science is a notable, worthy cause; however, a man in their right mind would be hard-pressed to agree that seeking immortality is a worthy use of one's time."

"It is not for you—or me—to decide that for Felicity." The sad lilt in her voice had Silas wondering if Mallory knew more of what went on in this room. "Not all things can be proved or disproved by scientific method."

Finally, she turned to him, but her eyes strayed to the stairwell behind him and the open door below before returning to meet his gaze. There was something there, just out of reach in her eyes, but Silas could not understand it.

Sorrow. Hurt. Defeat.

"I think it best I return downstairs before my aunt becomes concerned about my whereabouts."

"And find Miss Felicity?"

She shook her head, confusion clouding her hooded stare. "Yes, of course."

Silas did not dare take his stare from her. "You are returning home soon?"

"Aunt Hettie seeks to be at Blenheim Park before Christmastide."

"You do not want to go?" He sensed the hesitancy in her answer.

"It is not that." She drew her bottom lip between her teeth. "I rarely leave my family's estate, and I do so enjoy seeing Felicity. My visit has been far too short."

"But there will be other occasions to visit Tetbery."

"I fear not, my lord," Mallory said, clutching her gloved hands before her. "The duke is forcing Felicity to journey to London for a proper Season—to secure her a husband. This may very well be my last visit to the estate."

"I'm certain you've spoken to your friend to reassure her that London is not the awful fate she thinks it is," he prodded.

Her mouth drew downward, and her stare followed. "Unfortunately, I would not know what London and a proper Season entails beyond what I have heard from my mother or read about in the *London Daily Gazette*."

Why had he assumed she'd been introduced to polite society? As the only daughter of a wealthy and influential marquess, it would be foolish to assume Mallory hadn't been afforded a Season.

Then again, he'd never questioned the Marquess of Blandford's willingness to wed his daughter to a stranger either.

"You can show yourself out, my lord?" she asked.

"Certainly, but I shall walk you to the manor."

A hint of a smile settled on her lips. "We are *in* the manor." She tipped her head toward the wall behind her, and Silas noticed a nearly invisible seam in the stone. "I'll enter the house through the study."

The Tetbery Estate apparently held many secrets; however, Silas could not help but wonder if Lady Mallory hid far more.

"I best return to the village as my brother will be

arriving shortly." He grasped the handrail but made no move to turn. "Have a joyous Christmastide holiday. I look forward to our nuptials in the spring."

His heart stopped as he awaited her reply. He'd deceived her horribly, and she had every right to be angry with him. Continuing their betrothal was more than Silas deserved. But he was certain he wanted it.

"Of course, Silas," she mumbled before turning and hurrying toward the hidden door.

He watched in utter shock as she pulled a cord, and the door sprang open.

When she glanced back at him as she fled the room, he noticed her smile.

His reckoning was coming, and Silas greatly anticipated the day.

# CHAPTER 12

MALLORY STROLLED DOWN the walk in Bocka
Morrow, entering shops at random as she attempted to
keep her thoughts focused on things other than the
sensual dreams that had plagued her during the night.
She'd run into Felicity as she was leaving the laboratory,
and while her friend was upset, the Duke of Wycliffe
seemed to have the situation handled. She supposed her
vision had been correct, after all, about the two of them
growing closer.

The late-morning breeze off the ocean held a biting
chill; however, Mallory barely noticed it, and Aunt
Hettie had layered on two thick cloaks in preparation
for their trip into. Thus far, she'd purchased a new scarf
for her mother, an emerald necklace for Felicity, and a
new stationery set for their housekeeper in Launceston,
along with many other baubles for various servants at
both Tetbery and Blenheim.

Frankly, she was running out of time and coin.

And Aunt Hettie would not believe she had anyone
left to buy a gift for.

The streets were crowded with both local villagers
and many smartly dressed men and women, likely in

Cornwall for the wedding taking place tomorrow at the castle.

Oh, how Mallory wished to attend. She'd been invited, after all, and by the countess herself. Yet, when she'd shared the news with her aunt, the aging woman had only shaken her head and forbidden Mallory from attending. The only shining light…she hadn't barred Mallory from the Yule ball. That Mallory had failed to mention the celebration could be the reason.

"Auntie," Mallory cooed with a grin. "Look, a haberdashery. I am certain Tressa would adore a new set of ribbons for her hair."

When Aunt Hettie waved her off, Mallory entered the shop and feigned interest in an ivory *Scrimshaw* sewing kit displayed in the window. She did her best to appear interested in the many essentials being sold by the haberdasher, but her stare kept straying out the window to the town beyond.

One more day. Mallory had convinced Aunt Hettie to remain at Tetbery Estate for one more day.

Mallory was determined to use it wisely. Even from this vantage point, she had a clear view of The Crown & Anchor. Lord Lichfield hadn't so much as appeared in the several hours she and Aunt Hettie had wandered about town. Could it be the countess had offered him lodging at the castle and he no longer resided at the tavern?

*Damnation.* After the fright from the explosion in Felicity's lab had subsided, all Mallory could think about was Lord Lichfield, Silas, his lips on hers, his arms holding her close, and the surprising way her body fit against his. Their kiss had sparked something deep within her, and now she was helpless to think of anything else.

Though if Felicity or Aunt Hettie had noticed her distracted nature that morning, neither had commented on it.

"Will you be buying that, miss?" Mallory glanced

up to see the proprietor at her elbow gesturing to her hands. She'd removed the ivory sewing kit and now clutched it in her hands. "I can have it wrapped for you."

"Oh, it is lovely, and I was going to purchase it for a friend; however, I only now remembered she does not enjoy sewing as a pastime." Mallory returned the kit to its place in the window and smiled as the man moved on to another customer.

Glancing about the shop, Aunt Hettie was occupied, picking through a large bowl of pearl buttons while their footman had been sent back to the carriage a while ago with more packages to stow.

Staring out the window once more, Mallory searched the busy street for any sign of her betrothed. Certainly, he must leave the tavern soon, for there was absolutely no chance of Mallory convincing her aunt to dine in the public room at The Crown & Anchor. Perhaps she'd consider the notion if the establishment suggested was The Mermaid's Kiss, the proper lodging house farther away from the dock area. However, Silas hadn't secured a room there.

Maybe Mallory should give up on seeing Silas again before the spring.

But then, what if her vision came true and he didn't make it until the spring?

It would be Mallory's doing for not warning him.

"Are you ready, my girl?" Aunt Hettie shouted across the shop as she hefted a large box. "My feet will be in need of rest before long."

"Yes, Aunt Hettie." Mallory hurried over and took the box from her, tucking it under her arm. "You wanted to visit the apothecary shop before returning to Tetbery, correct?"

"Of course." From her aunt's shrill tone, Mallory suspected the woman had forgotten about needing her tonic that helped with the pain in her shoulders and knees. "I must stop at old Gustavo's while here. There is little telling when we will be back in Bocka Morrow."

When? Mallory was certain she meant *if*.

With the duke continuing to demand Felicity journey to London for a proper Season, they would not receive another invitation to stay at Tetbery.

She thought of Lord Lichfield and his family who lived at the castle not far from town. Perhaps after they wed, an invitation to visit the castle would be extended. Aunt Hettie could not even bring herself to exit the carriage at the old castle; it was highly unlikely she'd agree to lodge within.

With a sigh, Mallory followed her aunt from the shop and turned toward Gustavo's Apothecary Shoppe, and nearly collided with the one man she'd been hoping to see since waking that very morning from a deliciously sweet night filled with improper dreams.

SILAS WOULDN'T HAVE left Slade alone at the tavern if the need hadn't been great. His coat had been utterly ruined by smoke the day before, and he doubted even a proper laundress could remove the smell from the garment. Which meant Silas had two options: procure a new overcoat or freeze in the blasted cold.

Certainly an hour away from The Crown & Anchor wasn't time enough for Slade to find trouble—or worse, run up a sizable debt in the card room.

With his head down to protect his uncovered face and neck from the cold, he stepped around a woman who'd rudely taken to walking down the middle of the walkway, leaving not enough room for a grown man to pass on either side unless they turned sideways.

"Lord Lichfield?" Poised and properly attired, Lady Mallory stood before him—her gown of the lightest blue he'd ever seen, high-waisted with a bodice laced with small pearls that reflected the sun from above. Her hair was brushed and gathered at her shoulder with a small, unadorned hat perched securely atop her head. The large, wrapped package under her arm slipped slightly.

…and she smiled up at him.

"Lady Mallory." He turned slightly, not the least bit shocked it was Lady Hettie Hughes who took up a large portion of the walkway. "Lady Hettie. It is nice to see you both. I thought you'd be safely on your way to Blenheim Park by now."

Lady Hettie snorted. "Thought so myself, but Mallory desired another day at Tetbery, though I cannot see how she can handle this bone-chilling coastal air."

She glanced up at him from under hooded lids. "We are finishing a bit of holiday gift shopping before we return home."

Her cheeks blossomed with color, and there was little doubt she was picturing their embrace from the day before.

"Allow me to hold your package, my lady."

"It is not so heavy," she said. "We are to visit only one last shop and then return to our carriage."

"I am afraid I must insist." He reached for the box, and she gladly handed it over. "I can deliver it to your carriage while you continue shopping."

"Certainly kind of you, Lichfield," Lady Hettie said, her brow rising with suspicion.

"I will walk with him, Auntie, while you speak with Gustavo. If that is agreeable." He noted she kept her stare on Lady Hettie, not risking a glance in his direction. "We will deliver the package, and I shall return quickly to help you."

The old woman straightened her stooped shoulders to glare up at Silas. He gave her his most reassuring smile.

But when Lady Hettie's eyes darkened, he suspected she'd found no reassurance in his open grin.

"Very well, but do not dilly-dally, and come straight back."

Mallory leaned close and placed a quick kiss to her aunt's cheek. "Certainly, Aunt Hettie."

She waved them off and started for the apothecary shop down the walk.

"It is this way, my lord," Mallory said, gesturing in the opposite direction her aunt had started off in. "The carriage is only around the corner there."

He held out his arm to her, and she set her fingers lightly at the crook of his elbow.

"I hope all is well with Miss Felicity and her laboratory." Bloody hell. The last thing he wanted to speak of was another woman while Mallory was on his arm, but propriety demanded he ask after her friend. "Nothing was ruined in her lab, I hope."

She kept her gaze trained ahead of them, giving Silas the opportunity to admire her flawless, porcelain complexion and rounded button nose. "She had left the lab a few moments before. Turns out, no one in the manor heard the explosion but us. Nothing was damaged, and Felicity is free to continue her work."

"Very good," he mumbled.

"What of your evening, my lord," she inquired. "How did you fare?"

Yes, a much safer topic for discussion—on the surface, at least. "My brother arrived at sunset, and I have been getting him settled in Bocka Morrow. My aunt has insisted we attend the Yule ball at the castle tomorrow evening, and thus, I will be remaining in town a few more days."

"It must be nice to have your brother near."

"Well, it is better for all he is close where I can keep watch on him."

"You take much responsibility for your younger siblings," she commented. "Sometimes, I long to have a sibling—any sibling—close and underfoot."

"What of your brother, the Earl of Bristol? He is unwed, and a bit of a notorious gentleman about town, or so I've heard." It was all Silas could think of to distract her from conversation about his family. While his aunt had unknowingly exposed part of his secret, there was much more he didn't want her to know. "Does he not visit Blenheim often?"

They kept a slow pace as they walked, each knowing once their task was complete, he'd need return her to Lady Hettie without delay...and he would have no other cause to remain in her presence.

"I do not often see Adam or my father." She paused, adjusting her hold on his arm. "I see my mother frequently when my father can spare her accompaniment in London. However, it is normally only Aunt Hettie I have for company."

"A pity, Lady Mallory, I have come to enjoy your company." Not that they'd shared much time together, but she'd helped save him from the man outside the public house and kissed him with much vigor. Certainly, those two instances qualified as moments when he enjoyed her company. "Why not travel to London to be closer to family?"

She shook her head, her dark curls flowing over her shoulder to brush his arm. He only wished he could feel their soft, velvety strands through his linen shirt.

"There would be no one to keep Aunt Hettie company if I went to town; besides, my father is a very busy man with Parliament and would not have much time anyways. I am happy at Blenheim." Her listless tone spoke to the contrary.

Silas longed to ask her more, but they'd arrived at the Tetbery carriage where a footman took the box from him and stored it in the boot.

As they turned back toward the apothecary, he wondered if Lady Mallory didn't need this marriage as much as he did. Could they both be struggling to find something that had been missing thus far in their lives?

# CHAPTER 13

MALLORY'S DILEMMA OF how she'd get to the Yule ball at Keyvnor had been as easily remedied as her excuse for delaying their departure from Tetbery. The hours spent in Bocka Morrow yesterday had left Aunt Hettie with aching feet and the sniffles, as well as a groggy head, thus putting off their return home until the next morning.

It was all the reprieve Mallory would receive—and, hopefully, all she needed.

With Aunt Hettie under the weather in bed, and Felicity entertained elsewhere, Mallory had set about preparing herself for the ball. As she'd never attended a proper London soirée, especially one in celebration of a blessed union of two couples, she wasn't entirely certain of her attire. Years prior, she'd gone to a small country festival in Launceston, yet it was in no way as grand as the ball to take place at the castle. And if she were being honest, she'd only stood on the fringes of that gathering, never daring to join in the revelry.

This night was to be different.

Perhaps she would even be so bold as to dance with Silas…before everyone.

Gowned in a pretty green taffeta dress with a wide gold sash about her waist, Mallory had hurried down the stairs and out to the stables in hopes of securing a horse to ride to the castle. The journey was not far, and though it was cold, her cloak would keep the worst of the dirt from her dress. If she kept her head bent low over the horse's neck, the wind would not completely ruin her perfectly coiffured curls.

To her delight, the duke's carriage stood waiting, and the driver offered her transport to Castle Keyvnor. If he thought it peculiar that she was attending the ball alone, he spoke not a word of it. He'd likely already delivered Wycliffe to the castle. When he dropped her at the back of a line of carriages waiting to dispose of their own passengers, he'd promised to return for her later in the evening.

And so, Mallory found herself creeping about the outside of Castle Keyvnor, her back pressed against the rough stone wall.

She'd first thought to exit the carriage and walk directly into the castle—she'd been invited by the countess, after all. But then she'd spotted the gardens…a very familiar plot. She'd been plagued with déjà vu when she noticed the area before her meeting with the countess a few days prior, but under the bright Christmastide moon, the winter landscape was unmistakably the scene from her vision.

Now, her satin slippers were damp with evening dew, and her nose was frozen to the point of numbness. Dirt clung to the hem of her cloak, and her hood hadn't been enough to keep the wind from her hair. Her fingers were as stiff as the stone at her back.

But none of that mattered to Mallory.

This was where it would happen. This was where her vision would turn into reality, with the moon high and large overhead, and the deserted hedge maze in the near distance. Leafless branches hung low on an apple tree to the left, and a willow appeared frozen nearby.

Her heart stopped for a brief moment with fear that Silas had already met his fate and she was too late to warn him, but no. The music and merriment at her back drifting from the open veranda doors of the castle did not let on that a tragedy had yet taken place.

The ballroom was an utter crush, and locating Silas within would be nearly impossible.

There was no better place to wait than in the garden, to halt him before it happened.

It was the way things had to be. Silas needed to live, they must wed, and Mallory's visions for her own future would be proven wrong. An eternity alone, devoid of her own home and family was a fate worse than death for her. Mallory's years spent in solitude except for Aunt Hettie must come to an end. She could be content as Lord Lichfield's wife. If their time together had proven anything, it was that the earl was a kind and compassionate man, and a lord who cared for his family. Once she was his family, he would care for her just as he did for his siblings.

And there was no use denying she'd more than enjoyed their kiss outside Tetbery.

Sure they were not a love match and hadn't selected one another, but that did not prevent them from getting along amicably and having a family. Maybe even finding love someday. Many in England thrived in arranged marriages, coordinated by well-meaning and trusted family members who knew best when it came to determining the fate of future generations.

*Fate* had brought them together, and Mallory would be damned if she'd allow it to take him away before things came to fruition. She would tell him, in time, of her gift, and he could call it what he would: either a blessing or a curse.

As her indignation rose, so did it pump the blood through her veins and warm her.

No matter how much her family tried to convince her otherwise, it would weigh on her greatly if she did not speak to Silas and keep him from entering the garden.

As if her rambling mind had conjured him from thin air, Lord Lichfield hurried through the terrace doors and down the steps into the winter garden, glancing nervously over his shoulder the entire way as his boots sounded on the stone ground. He was running from something—or someone—but she hadn't seen that in her vision. She'd never seen him in such a frenzy; gone were his composed demeanor and the aristocratic tilt of his chin.

Uncertainty kept her frozen, remaining in her hiding spot against the castle wall as Silas moved farther into the garden, nearly to the hedge maze entrance. The vision she saw would not come to pass if he entered the maze.

If she were wrong, and he halted outside its entrance, he would be struck down in a matter of moments.

SILAS SLIPPED OUT the study door with a heavy sigh of relief. Everything was moving at lightning speed and was like a crushing weight on his shoulders. He'd never expected his mother's family to be so welcoming, inviting him and his brother into the castle with open arms and good cheer. Part of him wished he'd left Slade in town and brought Sybil. She would have greatly enjoyed meeting her cousins and attending the ball.

Unfortunately, he hadn't brought his sister but his twin.

Another of the reasons he'd found himself in the castle study. Slade had joined the tables in the card room almost immediately after their arrival. It was a friendly game with small bets being placed on the tables, and Silas doubted his brother could get into too much trouble over the course of a couple of hours. Yet, after only an hour's time, his brother had left the card room in a hurry with angry shouts in his wake.

Silas had extricated himself from the group he'd been speaking with but had lost his brother in the crush of people.

Pity the footman had taken his newly tailored coat upon his arrival, for the night had grown exceedingly cold since the sun set hours before.

Finally, the path led to the gardens bordering the castle, and the only place he'd yet to search for Slade. This was not how he'd thought to spend his evening, in pursuit of his rakehell twin. Certainly, he'd looked forward to making the acquaintance of more family, and in the deep recesses of his mind, he'd hoped Lady Mallory would attend. The countess had issued an invitation; however, Lady Hettie had spoken of her desire to return home. They were likely safely back at Blenheim Park as he stalked toward the winter landscape of the castle gardens.

The echo of footfalls drew Silas's attention, but they came not from the garden but above. Stepping back from the castle wall, he looked upward, thankful the moon was high and bright, illuminating the battlements and parapet lining the top of the castle and going from one tower to another. A man rushed along the path overhead, carrying a large box of sorts. What could the man possibly be doing up there at this hour?

There wasn't time to ponder that. Silas needed to find Slade and fix whatever trouble he'd caused. If he'd garnered a hefty debt, Silas would make good on it. Somehow.

It all happened too quickly. A burst of light green and gold darted out from the far side of the castle. Silas turned in that direction and spotted Slade standing close to the hedge maze. At the same time, a flash from above blinded him.

He rubbed at his eyes, attempting to bring everything back into focus and banish the colored spots blurring his sight as he pivoted back toward the garden.

Slade lay motionless on the ground.

And a woman—Lady Mallory?—ran toward him.

His heart stopped in his chest, and his lungs seized, preventing him from getting the air he needed to call out to them.

# CHAPTER 14

A SCREAM TORE from Mallory's throat, nearly bringing her to her knees as she desperately sought air to fill her lungs once more. When the loud crack had sounded, she ran toward him without a care for her own safety and allowed the winter night to cocoon her in its embrace. She'd been wrong, ever so wrong. There was no changing her visions, no altering fate, and undeniably no future happiness for her.

Still, her heart told her it might not be too late.

She could save him. Find out where the bullet had entered him and staunch the flow of blood.

It had to have been gunfire that brought him down. She'd noted the flash as if it were very close to her, but she couldn't stop to see who'd fired the weapon.

There was no time for that.

Perhaps her time had run out already.

"Lady Mallory!"

The shout was familiar, but she kept moving toward the figure crumpled only a scant few paces from the hedge maze. If he were still in danger, she would be at his side through it—for what else did she have if she lost him?

A family who would rather keep her hidden? A brother who outright detested her for something she could not control? An aunt who sheltered her from the world but truly had done more harm than good?

That could not be all that was meant for her.

It wasn't enough. It never had been.

But this man, Silas, had changed all of that when he offered for her hand. Oddly, he likely didn't realize he was saving her, just as she'd saved him at the tavern—the way she meant to save him today, if it was in her power. She would spend their entire lives *saving* him, if necessary.

"Mallory!" The voice finally broke through her determination, and she halted, turning toward whoever shouted for her. "Mallory, stop!"

It could not be. She would not believe it.

Silas stood no more than twenty paces away, his face ashen with fear.

She looked back at the man lying on the ground, noting his subtle movements.

In an instant—or perhaps it was longer—Silas was at her side.

"Silas…but…the vision," she mumbled, her entire body trembling as she gazed up into his familiar clear blue eyes. Her hands moved of their own accord to cup his smooth cheeks. He was real and standing before her. "Who—what—I was wrong, dreadfully wrong."

"Shhhh." Silas kept a hold of her, his comforting voice bringing a calm she'd never known. "It is only Slade, my brother, he is likely on one of his larks. And what is this mention of visions?"

"He is not shot?" Her voice was shrill, her throat burning from her earlier scream. When he shook his head and gestured toward the fallen man—Silas's brother—she noticed him pushing to his feet. "Twins?"

She'd witnessed the scene through Silas's eyes, not her own. It was his vision she'd seen, not a prediction of her own fate.

As a pair, they moved to Slade. The resemblance to Silas was shocking. The only difference of note was Slade's hair. It was cut shorter and did not have the unruly curls Silas favored.

"Slade," Silas growled, keeping her close to his side. "What is the meaning of this?"

The man's sheepish grin was as dissimilar to his brother's severe smile as his sheared locks. "I found I lost a hefty amount at the tables and needed a quick exit before Lord St. Giles came calling for my debts."

"You've been at Keyvnor for no more than two hours." Silas released her long enough to scrub at this face. "How is that possible?"

"Not my night, dear brother, not my night. Besides, I wouldn't put it past St. Giles to open fire on me. Thought it in my best interest to play dead, as it were."

"You thought it in your best interest to what?" Irritation laced Silas's tone, and his brow drew low further darkening the night as anger rolled off him in waves, much like the sea battering the cliffs at Tetbery.

Slade finally noted Mallory, his stare taking her in from head to toe as he responded to his brother. "You know, let the man think he got me."

"You are incorrigible." Silas's exasperation was evident.

"Yes, but that is why I am so bloody sought-after," he said with a chuckle as he stared at the terrace behind them. "Speaking of which, I best be going before St. Giles finds me here." With a quick bow, he turned to her. "Lady Mallory Hughes, I presume?"

"Yes." Her voice quaked, and she took a deep, steadying breath before continuing. "That is I."

"Your resemblance to your sibling is also remarkable," Slade crowed before turning and rushing toward the hedge maze.

"Wait!" she shouted. "You know my brother?"

"I may owe him a quid…or five hundred," Slade threw over his shoulder with a shrug as he disappeared into the maze.

Mallory stood silently at Silas's side long after his twin had disappeared from sight, the fog of their warm breaths mingling in the cold December air. At some point, the evening chill had fled, and a heat now surrounded her.

It finally hit her then, Silas had touched her face, held her gaze, and no vision had invaded. She'd sensed it coming, waited for it to slam into her conscious, but something in his stare had kept her grounded in the present, not some alternate future.

"Tell me of these visions…"

Mallory kept her eyes trained on the maze when she spoke for fear his interest would quickly turn to disgust, and he draw away from her. "When I come into contact with people—skin-to-skin—or touch objects, I see things. Things that have yet to happen, but will in the future."

"And you saw this moment with Slade?" he asked.

"Yes, when you and I touched that first day at Tetbery—"

"Your eyes?" It was a question he did not wait for her to answer. "They cloud, turn a deep grey as if a storm rolls over your sight."

"You noticed?" It was then she turned to him. His spoke with near reverence, not the sickened tones others used when speaking of her skill, not that more than a handful of people had been trusted with their family *affliction*. "My father begged me not to speak of it until after we were wed." She turned away from him then, ashamed she'd agreed to dupe Silas. "I understand if my curse is—"

Silas lifted his hand, caressing her arm before pushing back her hood. "It is not a curse. It is a gift…a very special, awe-inspiring gift."

"Not according to my family," she confessed.

"Then they are not looking upon the situation with open eyes." His finger lifted her chin until their eyes met. "What have you seen of our future?"

She knew her eyes clouded with his question—not with a coming vision but sorrow, defeat.

"Come now, tell me." His thumb lightly caressed her cheek.

"In every vision of my future, which I see only through touching those close to me, I am alone." It was gut-wrenching to admit. "But our betrothal gave me hope for a different outcome."

"And who says you're destined to continue down the path those have envisioned for you?"

"My visions have never proven false before tonight. And even with that, it was not completely inaccurate," Mallory said, shrugging. She could not let Silas know how much she prayed the visions would not come true.

"Then I think it is up to us to change the path fate has set for you." He drew her close, their bodies pressed together, melding as if she belonged there, in Silas's embrace. "Would you like to know what I think on the matter?"

"I think I would," she whispered into the night, her stare holding his. If she looked away, perhaps this moment would disappear as if it had never come to pass. She could not stand to live with that.

"I think," he started, pausing to place a kiss on her forehead, "we are bound by far more than our betrothal agreement. We will not be held apart by someone else's vision of our future. With only the Christmastide moon above, and you and I below, I promise to give you the future you seek. I can promise you a home—several homes, if that's what you wish—a family, and me. If that is enough…"

"More than enough." It was as if he'd read her mind, knew the things she longed for most, and promised to give all he possessed to make her not just content in their marriage but happy.

"That is, if you can look past Slade's rakehell ways

and are fond of troublesome young girls who ask too many questions," he continued in a rush.

"You need not convince me, my lord," she said with a smile. "Even without the signed betrothal, I believe you are correct. We are bound under the Christmastide moon."

"My family is not extensive—" he paused, glancing toward the castle. "—well, until recently, I haven't thought my family larger than my siblings and mother, which is not much to offer, but they are kind people. Loving and caring. They will support you—us, in whatever future we decide to embark on. I may not have unlimited funds as most men of the *ton*, but we shall live comfortably—in London, or at Ditchley Hall, if you prefer."

It was more than she'd ever dreamed possible for her future.

Above them, a sudden glow caught her notice—the moon, it was as if it had brightened, acknowledging the truth Silas spoke and binding them together ever the more.

It was then it hit her…with more force than any vision had.

"My home, our home, will be wherever we are together, be it London or your country estate." There was no fear with Silas at her side. If he deemed London was where they needed to be, then she would be there with him. If he preferred a quiet existence in Hampshire, so be it. He would never allow any harm to come to her, and she'd already promised herself to care and watch over him. "I will follow you anywhere."

He shook his head, and Mallory feared she'd misspoke. "No."

"No?" She knew her face paled for he leaned close, his hands cupping her face once more.

"No, I'd prefer you stand at my side—my partner in all matters, not follow my lead."

Not follow his lead, Mallory pondered.

Pushing to her tiptoes, she asked, "Do you truly mean that, my lord?"

When he nodded, Mallory pressed her lips to his, their bodies drawing close—his arousal evident in the way his hard length pressed against her belly, even through the layers of clothes, she felt every glorious inch of him.

Oh, though theirs was a marriage of convenience—managed and arranged by others—Mallory had little doubt it would also be a love match.

The Christmastide moon as her witness, Mallory would love this man for as long as fate allowed her breath.

# CHAPTER 15

*April 1812*

MALLORY SAT IN the atrium at Ditchley Hall, allowing her eyes to drift shut and a smile to settle on her lips. The humid air and scent of budding blossoms was her solace for the morning as servants scurried about the estate in preparation for her wedding to Silas.

She set her pruning shears on the workbench beside the sack of soil she'd carried in from the old, decaying shed in the far corner of the lawn area without opening her eyes. The room, with its many varieties of plants and flowers, had become one of her favorite spots at Silas's country estate since she and Aunt Hettie had become regular visitors after they departed Cornwall.

Servants and family alike gave her time and solitude during the early hours of the day.

Sybil, Silas's precocious younger sister, feared what the humid air did to her ebony locks. Slade was more often than not in London—or the local tavern in search of a wager. Aunt Hettie's knees made it nearly impossible for her to move through the cluttered atrium.

Odd that she'd come to think of Sybil and Slade as family. They'd eagerly stepped into the roles of doting brother—Slade—and eager-to-please sister—Sybil. Mallory was happy for their welcoming nature and the opportunity to be a part of an actual family. They cared naught about her peculiar ways, nor judged her for her tendency to shy away from the unknown.

Since the new year passed, Aunt Hettie and she had come to think of Ditchley Hall as *home*.

Mallory sighed, opening her eyes and returning to her task as footsteps sounded on the cobblestone floor. The solid, confident stride was one she'd come to know—very well—over the past several months.

Silas.

Only he dared invade her brief hours of quiet.

His steps stopped directly behind her, and his hands settled at her shoulders, gently caressing. In quick order, his lips pressed to the sensitive spot behind her ear.

"Are you certain this is what you want?" he mumbled, trailing his lips down her neck.

The intimacy sent a shiver through Mallory and was likely one of the reasons she continued to visit the atrium each morning. Without fail, Silas came to her, and they were afforded a few moments, sometimes hours, of privacy before anyone came looking for them. If Aunt Hettie suspected their secret rendezvous spot, she mentioned nothing of it to Mallory.

"I am certain." In truth, besides her commitment and budding love for Silas, there was nothing she was more certain of.

"It was much for Sybil to ask." He straightened behind her, and the warmth of his lips at her skin receded.

"I am to be your wife—a countess, no less—and it will be partly my duty to see that Sybil's debutante Season is a crush." Mallory had never thought she'd readily agree to spend any time in London, let alone chaperoning and sponsoring Silas's youngest sibling. Yet, when the girl had begged her to journey to town during the height of the Season, Mallory was helpless to do anything but agree. "Besides, I must familiarize myself with town life…it is long past time."

"What about your…" His voice trailed off, and they both knew what he spoke of.

"They hardly come anymore, and none since our time in Cornwall has been the least bit unsettling," Mallory said, setting her shears down and turning to face Silas. It was another peculiar occurrence. Her visions had receded, only invading every few weeks. And they spoke of happy years to come. Was it Silas whose presence kept the visions at bay? "With your mother returning to France after the wedding, even with your aunts' assistance, Sybil needs a familiar face by her side."

"And you are to be that familiar face." He leaned down, placing a kiss to her forehead. "Yet, I cannot think to allow you to compromise your well-being to accommodate my family."

"*Our* family," Mallory proclaimed, stepping back to look up into his clear blue eyes.

"Yes, our family," he said with a chuckle.

"How is Lady Lichfield faring?" Mallory asked, hesitantly.

"She still remains in her private chamber, but has allowed Aunt Regina to visit," Silas confided. "I think she is counting down the days until her return to Paris."

"It is where she is comfortable, and we cannot deny her that." Silas's mother was an enigma that was not easily understood. The woman was almost childlike in demeanor and preferred her own company to that of others. Even Aunt Hettie had found it difficult to draw the woman out. "Aunt Hettie has spoken of your mother, and her happiness in Paris. She will be taken care of, and we shall visit when it is safe."

Silas wrapped his arms around Mallory and pulled her close. "Yes, I would like that very much."

"That is very good, because I must insist we see Mary Louisa as often as possible."

"When are your parents arriving?"

"Mother sent word to Aunt Hettie that they'd be arriving today, likely before late afternoon." It was the only unease that hadn't been banished during the months spent getting to know Silas and his family. His family had been more than welcoming to her and Aunt Hettie. Mallory would go so far as to say that she'd grown closer to Slade and Sybil than she'd ever been with her own brother, Adam. "They will stay only two days and then return to London."

"That is likely for the best. However, we will journey to town next month." Silas was determined to set to rights Mallory's strained relationship with the marquess and marchioness, though Mallory had stated it was not something to hedge one's bets on—as Slade commonly phrased it. "Oh, and I came in search of you for a reason."

"Other than a few stolen kisses?" she teased, thankful the conversation had steered in another direction. "Because I am not sure I can spare a moment if—"

Silas captured her lips, cutting her words short.

And Mallory could think of no other place she longed to be, and no other man she desired to be there with.

It was still inconceivable that they'd found one another despite their different upbringings.

Yet, with time, their bond had only grown stronger and deeper, defying everything Mallory had feared her future would hold.

Silas sighed, their lips parting, and a frown creasing his face. "While I would relish nothing more than to remain here in the atrium with you until our morning nuptials, I fear we cannot."

An inkling of dread crept down her spine. "Why ever not, my lord?"

"Because, our honored guest has arrived, and I cannot think of anything more fitting than to parade our love before the man, as he was fairly certain I would muck things up long before now."

Her stomach fluttered, and her heart raced at his mention of love. Swallowing hard, she said, "Surely, he was not so rude as to say that..."

"But he was thinking it, I assure you," he replied with a wink.

"Then by all means, let us not tarry, and rush to greet the esteemed Mr. Horace Peabody to welcome him to Hampshire." Their mutual family solicitor had been the source of much merriment over the past several months. Mallory had discovered he'd been the lone man privy to both Mallory's secrets and that of the Lichfield family; yet, he'd championed their match. She was greatly looking forward to making the man's acquaintance at long last. When Silas moved to her side and offered his arm, Mallory slipped hers through his without a second of hesitation. "I suppose we owe Mr. Peabody our most sincere gratitude, do we not?"

"I guess it is only his due," Silas said, straightening his shoulders. "Though, I am hesitant to abandon our solitude, even for Mr. Peabody."

Mallory patted his arm, her light laughter echoing in the vaulted room.

As they approached the door that led into the main house, the frame shuddered as it swung open, crashing into the wall behind it. Slade skidded into the atrium, his boots slipping in a puddle created when Mallory had given the plants their morning watering.

"What in the bloody hell?!" Silas immediately pushed Mallory behind him as if preparing for danger. "Slade, why are you panting so hard? And your pants look as if you've rolled in the muck in the stables."

Mallory pushed from safety and laughed once

more. "Yes, Slade," she echoed. "What are you up to now?"

To his credit, Slade gained his balance and bowed to his future sister, but could not quite keep his attention focused on Mallory or Silas, his stare straying over his shoulder. "Good morn, my lady. Brother."

Silas waved off the man's attempt at pleasantries. "Did you hide Lady Hettie's needlepoint again?" When Slade's chest puffed as if offended at the accusation, Silas continued, "Put flour in Sybil's face powder?"

"Of course not, dear brother, I learned my lesson well where Sybil is concerned."

"Then what has you breathing hard and fleeing as if the Devil is on your tail?" Mallory questioned.

"The Devil," Slade mused, rubbing at his chin. "Yes, I think we can all agree the Devil has arrived at Ditchley Hall."

"What in the blazes does that mean?" Silas's voice thundered, and the windowpanes quaked in response, yet Slade seemed unaffected by his elder brother's demand.

"By the way, the Devil goes by the moniker Earl of Bristol." Slade's voice dropped to a whisper as if saying the name would conjure the man. "I must be going before he finds me here and demands my soul!"

Mallory couldn't help but find the irony in Slade's proclamation. It had never crossed her mind to think of her brother, Adam, as the Devil; however, Slade's words held merit. "Come now, my brother would not dare cause injury while staying as a guest at Ditchley Hall. Besides, any outstanding debt owed to my brother has been discussed and satisfied."

Unease prickled at the nape of Mallory's neck when Slade turned his focus to the ground at his feet.

"Slade," Silas growled. "What are you not telling us?"

"Well"—he cleared his throat before bringing his eyes back to Mallory and Silas—"it appears I have incurred another debt with Bristol, and he means to collect it—or a pound of flesh, as it goes."

"Another debt—" Exasperation laced Silas's words.

"Tell us that is not so." Mallory sighed, fearing Adam's need for justice.

"'Fraid so. Must be going before he stumbles upon me again." Slade winked at Mallory as he slipped past and ducked low as he moved toward the rear of the atrium and the safety of the expansive gardens beyond.

"I did warn you about the precocious girl and scoundrel of a brother, did I not?" Silas mumbled.

"Well, I suppose it is only fair we both claim our unconventional families." Mallory paused, turning into Silas's embrace and staring into his intense, cerulean eyes. "However, no matter their strangeness, it does not change how I feel about you."

His brow arched high. "Tell me, Lady Mallory, how do you feel about me?"

Did she dare say the word?

Perhaps Silas thought it too soon—or too ambitious for this connection at this point.

Yet, there was no denying it was there…a love that bound them together.

"Silas, I love you. That is the only word sufficient to express my feelings for you." She didn't dare look away or break eye contact, for she wished to know where his heart lay.

The smile that spread across his face brightened even the darkest corner of the atrium, though late-morning light pierced the windowpanes on all three sides.

Mallory held her breath, and waited; though Silas did not let her wait long.

"I believe that is the only term I can use, as well." He brought his hands to cup her cheeks, and suddenly, she was standing in the middle of Castle Keyvnor's gardens again, the cold December night sending a chill through her and banishing the humid air of the atrium. "I love you, Mallory."

# AUTHOR'S NOTES

Thank you for reading *Bound by the Christmastide Moon!*

If you enjoyed *Bound by the Christmastide Moon,* be sure to write a brief review at any retailer.

I'd love to hear from you!
You can contact me at:
Christina@christinamcknight.com

Or write me at:
P.O. Box 1017
Patterson, CA 95363

www.ChristinaMcKnight.com
Check out my website for giveaways, book reviews, and information on my upcoming projects,
or connect with me through social media at:
Twitter: @CMcKnightWriter
Facebook: www.facebook.com/christinamcknightwriter
Goodreads: www.goodreads.com/ChristinaMcKnight

Sign up for my newsletter here:
http://eepurl.com/VP1rP

**Turn the page for an excerpt from**
***The Lady Loves A Scandal,***
**featuring Silas' sister Sybil and her love Gideon!**

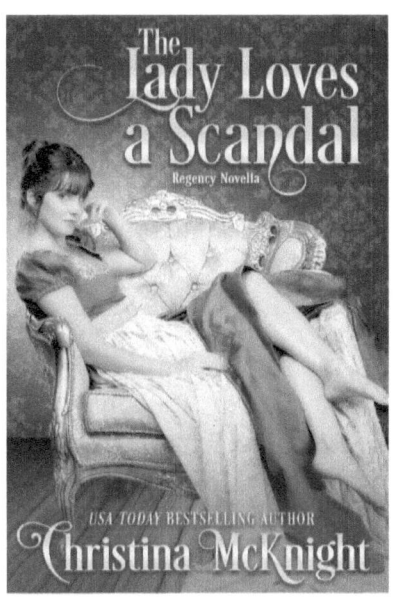

*After nearly a year of courtship, I, Lady X, am fairly confident in announcing the betrothal of one Viscount Galway of Barrow Burn, Northumberland to Lady Sybil Anson, most recently of London, by way of Paris, France and sister to the newly entitled Eighth Earl of Lichfield. As you, my dear readers, may remember, Lady Sybil is new to town after spending her childhood in the city of love. This author can do naught but imagine the draw between the stoic, reserved Lord Galway, and the young, impish foreigner, Lady Sybil. I am certain all of society will agree, both Lady Sybil and Lord Galway come with sordid pasts.*

~ LADY X, 10 February 1815

LADY SYBIL ANSON crouched ever lower until her rounded bottom nearly touched the rough, wooden slats of the floor of the hackney, her elbow resting precariously near a grease-covered metal piece. The constant jostle of the ramshackle conveyance as it moved leisurely through the crowded London streets was enough to loosen the pins securing her long tresses and sent shooting pains up her back to her neck. Certainly, a proper lady of the ton would never have used extreme trickery on her maid, fled her home under cover of night, traversed the dangerous alleys of London until she reached a well-traveled area of Regent Street, and hailed the first hack she spotted…all while keeping her hood pulled low, and the hem of her gown pulled high off the filth littering the streets.

Though no one claiming even a speck of good sense would ever describe Lady Sybil as proper.

Peculiar, maybe.

Entrusted with an odd sense of humor, commonly.

A lover of scandal, certainly.

However, it wasn't that she was any more unusual than other debutantes, or in possession of a dryer wit than many men of her acquaintance. The main difference was that she saw no need to mask her true self.

Cast the blame on her upbringing in France; her finicky, absentminded mother; or the fact that her older brother raised her. Whatever the reason, Sybil stood silently by as others used her past as fodder during her first Season.

Little did any of them know that Lady Sybil Anson did not give a bloody fig about their staunchly held beliefs on the ways a proper English miss should conduct herself while in polite company.

The hack turned a sharp corner, sending her

sprawling to the far side, her wrist and knee slamming against the high, wooden rail.

"Damnation and hellfire," she muttered. She flexed her fingers and rotated her wrist to test the damage.

Pushing back to her seat, Sybil was encouraged to see they'd finally entered Grosvenor Square, where the roads were not riddled with potholes, and the evening traffic was sparse. Unfortunately, with the affluent neighborhood also came increased illumination from the row of townhouses flanking her on both sides of the street. Before departing her home, Sybil had made certain her hood shielded her from view and hid her long, dark hair. Even the sleeves of her cloak hung past her fingertips, the hem likewise long.

The guise was not to stay above scandalous gossip.

It was not her name—or that of her brothers—she worried over.

Blessedly, the hack slowed and turned once more, this time into a well-manicured circular drive, shadowed from above by the looming stone edifice of the Galway Townhouse.

"Stop here, sir," Sybil called. The command earned her a questioning glance from the driver. "I have no plans to draw you into any unsavory dealings, I promise you."

She knew the townhouse before her very well. Far better than any unwed lady should know a lord's London home. If anyone were to ask, she'd deny ever stepping foot into Galway Townhouse without her aunt or another relation as her chaperone.

That Lady Sybil proclaimed herself in love with Gideon Lyndon, Viscount Galway, meant little to the gossips about London. That she was certain he held a tender for her as well was also of little import—at least until the betrothal contracts were signed.

It made little sense that her being outside Gideon's home after dusk with no chaperone would be taken as proof of her ruined status and have scandalous repercussions on her family's already tarnished name. But in less than a day's time, after the contracts were duly signed and witnessed, a minor indiscretion between betrothed couples could be overlooked. And people thought her peculiar.

It made Sybil miss her time in Paris all the more. Days and nights spent free from worry over societal ridicule. People, young women included, given the opportunity to explore themselves and the city without fear of scandal. There were still rules to be followed, of course, but nothing as crushing and oppressive as her British counterparts.

She shook her head at the thought. No, not her British counterparts. Her country, her home, her future.

"Ye get'n down, miss?" the driver hissed in a hushed whisper. "I got me other fares ta earn."

"I need you to wait for me." Sybil smoothed her cloak over her gown, made certain her hood was high, and checked the driveway for onlookers—it was abandoned, at least for the moment. "I will not be overlong—" At the driver's hesitant stare, she continued. "And I shall pay triple your usual rate."

She'd known the man would agree long before he nodded in concurrence.

Another lesson she'd learned during her time in London.

With the right amount of funding, anything was possible—the finest gowns by the most sought-after modistes, the agreement of kept secrets, the quashing of gossip, and London hackney drivers willing to pick up and deliver any passenger without question.

It likely also helped that her brother was the Earl of Lichfield and wed to the daughter of a wealthy marquess, eccentric as her new sister-in-law may be.

"Lovely." Sybil stood, pulling her sleeves down to cover her gloves as she took hold of the side of the conveyance and swung her leg over the rail, finding the large wheel with her foot before bringing her other leg over to join the first as she hopped to the cobbled drive. Clapping her hands together to remove any dirt, Sybil turned a bright smile on the driver. "Thank you, sir."

His birdlike eyes widened, and he appeared almost impressed by her resourcefulness.

Sybil's mother referred to her daughter's practicality in all matters as gumption.

Another thing lacking in every London debutante she'd met—and even some men.

Another carriage rattled down the street behind her as the wind increased, pulling at her hood and the hem of her cloak. The moist, earthy aroma on the breeze foretold the coming rain, which was likely to fall sometime during the early morning hours and reduce to a light drizzle by first light.

Sybil wrapped her arms around her midsection, determined to be safely home and abed before the first drops assaulted the filthy London streets. She made her way along the hedge to a shadowed area at the side of Lord Galway's townhouse. The small, cobblestoned space was blocked from view—neither a passing coach nor the butler at the front door would spy them. Even if someone knew they were present, the darkened alcove masked them entirely.

The racing of her heartbeat at moments like these was fairly addicting.

The risk, the intrigue, the barely contained need that boiled inside her…

Sybil sped up as she moved down the hedge, arriving at the spot where she'd told Gideon to meet her. A part of her feared this excitement would fade once they were officially betrothed—not to mention once the wedding took place. Certainly, their adventure would continue even when they no longer had to sneak about town to see one another without a proper chaperone.

Holding her breath, she waited, certain she'd hear the familiar, solid footsteps that were Gideon's trademark. He was confident, though never arrogant. He was kind, yet never with an air of pity. He was stoic, but Sybil knew the man beneath the dour, reserved facade.

The minutes passed, and a spike of anxiety coursed through her. Had Oliver, the bookseller, gotten her message to Gideon in time? Was the viscount in residence this evening, or had he gone to his club, never knowing she wished to meet?

A tendril of doubt wormed its way into her thoughts.

Doubt. A funny emotion—and one that never pertained to Lord Galway.

He was dependable to a fault, unlike so many other things in Sybil's life.

She released a heavy sigh when, finally, his heavy footfalls sounded on the cobbled drive, moving in her direction.

"Sybil?" his deep baritone was almost disapproving and menacing in the darkness. "It is after midnight. What are you doing gallivanting about the dangerous city? I thought Mr. Oliver quite mad when he delivered your note earlier."

Her heart, only moments before racing with anticipation, almost stopped when Gideon stepped into the shadows with her, throwing his arms wide to greet her. Without thought, she rushed into his waiting embrace.

"I had to see you, Gideon," Sybil gushed, perturbed by the weakness evident in her voice.

"I will be round tomorrow—or, I suppose, later today—to sign the contracts."

"Are you certain?" Even after their yearlong courtship, Sybil feared Gideon would change his mind. Cry off…leave her.

"Of course," Gideon said, his words clipped, but he pulled her closer still and tucked her head under his chin. "The negotiations are complete. Everything is finalized except our signatures on the paperwork. I am to arrive on the morrow at eleven sharp. I anticipate that everything will be official by noon."

"Silas has forbidden me to join you until it is time to put my name to the agreements."

"It is the way of things, my love." Her heart skipped a beat at the endearment, but she pulled back from his embrace, and he rubbed his hands up and down her arms as if he could impart a bit of warmth. "Business is handled by men, though that does not mean I value your input any less."

"I think you appreciate more than my input, my lord," Sybil said coyly.

"I value much about you, my lady."

"Like what?" She couldn't help but provoke him. It was in these private moments that Gideon allowed his usual stoic exterior to crumble and fall—at least for a few moments. "Tell me, or I shall remain here all night."

"Your complex musings," he said with a smile, leaning forward and placing a kiss on her forehead. Sybil couldn't halt her giggle. "Your enchanting brown eyes."

"My mud puddle murky eyes, you mean?" It was their game, and Sybil allowed her lids to slide shut. Gideon placed a kiss on each.

"Your button nose that is usually stuck somewhere it does not belong," he mumbled before pressing his lips to the tip of said appendage. "And your rosebud-red lips."

When he didn't immediately kiss her, Sybil opened her eyes and gazed up into his light gray stare.

Heat pooled at the junction of her thighs.

Part of her hated that Gideon could bring her so quickly to desire while he remained seemingly unaffected.

"You are a poet, my lord," she whispered.

"And you are the enchantress who feeds all my poetic ramblings," he countered.

"I love you, Gideon Lyndon," she confessed,

pushing to her tiptoes until their lips were a mere inch apart. "I cannot wait until the day I am Viscountess Galway."

"Would you love me as much if I were a..." He paused, pursing his lips in thought. "A fishmonger? Or a vendor in Hyde Park or at Covent Gardens?"

"Would you risk your reputation as a gentleman to meet me in a darkened drive if I were an orange seller outside the theatre?"

"Yes," they both chimed in unison.

"Let us hope we never test those fates." Sybil laughed.

His reserved veneer returned as his eyes searched hers. Sybil was uncertain what he hoped to find.

"It was highly improper and unsafe for you to journey out tonight," he scolded. "What if something had happened? Or worse yet, you were taken and disappeared?"

Sybil grinned up at him. "Come now, Gideon, for all the talk of London's perilous streets, I know not of a single person being taken—especially the sister of an earl, the soon-to-be betrothed lady of a viscount."

His eyes darkened as he stepped back from her, his head shaking.

"We have met in similar ways the entirety of our courtship," she chided. "I am still whole."

Sybil patted her chest to prove she was unscathed, yet her attempt at dispelling his unease did naught to return them to their previous light banter.

"We have convened in a shielded grove in Hyde Park, at the bookseller off Bond, and outside both our homes, but never, ever so close to the witching hour." He pressed his lips to hers, but it was not their usual sweet kiss. His lips were firm and almost punishing. "If anything ever happened to you, I would not be able to go on."

He held her stare until she consented, "I will do nothing so foolish again."

His lips softened, and the hint of a smile returned. "Although, I can admit having you at my home—at least, outside my home—at such an hour, brings many scandalous thoughts to mind."

"Oh, do tell—"

A horse whinnied close by, and Sybil glanced over her shoulder to see the mare tied to the hack as it stepped from foot to foot and tossed its head back with another neigh.

"I should go," Sybil said.

"I will accompany you home." Gideon glanced toward his townhouse. "Allow me to summon my carriage."

Placing her gloved hand on his arm, Sybil called for him to wait. "Your coach could be seen, and that would lead to scandal. What if someone saw? I promised I would not bring any disgrace upon you."

"I cannot, in good conscience, allow you to—"

"I made it here without incident, my lord," she rushed to say.

"Be that as it may—"

The deafening sound of horses' hooves pierced the air, sending the hack's mare into another bout of distress as a lone man on horseback raced into Gideon's drive. The rider pulled to a halt mere feet from the front door, and Sybil feared for a moment that he was set on riding right through the wooden portal.

Gideon stiffened before her.

"Are you expecting someone?" Sybil asked.

Had her brothers discovered her missing? Had her maid returned to Sybil's chambers to check on her mistress, found her not in residence, and alerted the entire household?

Sybil sighed in relief when the man dismounted and stepped into the pool of light cast by the torches hung outside Gideon's door.

"Wait here," Gideon demanded, but he did not await her reply as he stalked from the shadows and addressed the rider, stopping him before the man pounded his clenched fist on the door.

The men stood close as they talked in hushed whispers that were carried away on the night breeze before they reached Sybil.

Finally, Gideon nodded and motioned for the man to go inside as he turned and started back toward Sybil.

Halting before her Gideon asked, "Are you certain you will be safe to return home alone?"

Suddenly, Sybil wasn't sure at all, but she would risk the unimaginable to avoid admitting that she'd been wrong to depart her home at midnight for their final clandestine meeting before their betrothal was officially announced.

Not trusting her voice to remain steady, Sybil bobbed her chin up and down.

"Good," he sighed. "I will see you on the morrow. Dream joyfully in your slumber."

"Who is the man?" she dared ask. "He seemed rather urgent in his arrival."

"It is nothing to worry about," Gideon said, but it did little to ease her apprehension. "Only a long-standing matter I've been attempting to rectify for some time."

Sybil's brow pulled low. If Gideon had hidden something from her before she hadn't noticed. But she was not foolish enough to think that a man arriving during the middle of the night was of no consequence. Questioning Gideon further would gain her nothing, however, unless she wished to start their betrothal with the mark of a nagging woman.

Gideon pulled her into his arms as his finger traced down her cheek and along her jawline. A shiver raced the length of her spine, and she pressed her body against his.

Soon enough, they'd be free to touch, caress, and kiss one another to their hearts' content, but for now, Sybil needed to return home before anyone noticed her missing. Besides, Gideon obviously had other matters to attend to before meeting with Sybil's brother in the morning.

"Farewell, my love."

"Until later." Sybil grinned up at him, determined not to allow the man waiting inside the Galway Townhouse to ruin this moment for her.

Rising to her tiptoes again, Gideon's lips met hers in the dark, and their mouths moved in a rhythmic rightness that always seemed present when she and the viscount were together.

It was rather advantageous she'd fallen in love with a man her family not only approved of, but whom society also held in high regard; although, even if Gideon were the son of a tailor, Sybil would love him still.

He broke away from her. "Now, hurry home."

With a final laugh and smile for her soon-to-be betrothed, Sybil turned and ran to the waiting hack, climbing back up without any assistance.

"Hanover Square, please," she called after taking her seat. She would do all in her power to remain safe— and that meant risking being sighted when the driver deposited her before her brother's townhouse. "Dering Street."

As they pulled away from Gideon's drive, she glanced over her shoulder. A groom had come from the stables and was nodding vigorously in response to whatever the viscount said.

Something was amiss. Sybil was certain of it, even if Gideon thought her concerns were eased.

"Pull over here," she called, her voice rising above the clop of the mare's hooves and the creaking of the hack wheels. When the driver did not immediately heed her command, she yelled. "Stop. Here. Please. Stop now."

Relenting, the driver pulled up on the reins.

Sybil turned to face Gideon's drive, the

neighboring properties now blocking his house from view.

"Miss," the driver said, not bothering to hide his irritation. "It be late."

"Do shush." Sybil held her finger to her lips. "Only a few more moments, I promise."

If the late-night visitor had only come about a business matter, he would leave in quick order, allowing Gideon to find his bed. The seconds ticked by, turning into minutes as the night wind howled down the street, trapped between the rows of townhouses on both sides.

The driver passed the reins from hand to hand, and the resounding jingle was nearly masked by the wind.

Sybil kept her eyes trained on the drive a few houses back.

Finally, the sound of hooves rang out once more on the cobbled ground as not one but two horses raced from Gideon's driveway and headed in the opposite direction of her stalled carriage.

One was the lone horseman from before, but the other…

Sybil's breath stuck in her throat, her lungs burning as she attempted to swallow.

The ebony horse accompanying the other rider was Goliath, Lord Galway's prized stallion.

She was helpless to do aught but watch the pair ride off into the night.

**Coming soon in print, audiobook, and e-book!**

# ABOUT THE AUTHOR

*USA TODAY* Bestselling Author Christina McKnight writes emotional and intricate Regency Romance with strong women and maverick heroes.

Her books combine romance and mystery, exploring themes of redemption and forgiveness. When she's not writing, Christina enjoys trying new coffeehouses, visiting wine bars, traveling the world, and watching television.

**Email:** Christina@ChristinaMcKnight.com
**Follow her on Twitter:** @CMcKnightWriter
**Keep up to date on her releases:**
www.christinamcknight.com
**Like Christina's FB Author page:**
ChristinaMcKnightWriter

www.ingramcontent.com/pod-product-compliance
Lightning Source LLC
Chambersburg PA
CBHW030537130626
46552CB00006B/2294